WHEN THE BARD CAME VISITING

KATHRYN ROSSATI

Author's Note

Dear readers,

Firstly, thank you for picking up this book! Secondly, I wanted to say that the stories featured in this collection are a compilation of my shorter works from the past seven years, in which I explored many different genres and styles of writing—and had enormous fun doing so.

"The Poison Spreading", "The Lowlands", "Flight in the Dark", "Miko's Courage" and "A New Family" were originally written for a project aiming to educate readers on both the causes and effects of deforestation, and though sadly the project had to be put aside due to other commitments, I chose to include them here because—well—I like them. I thought you might, too.

I did take great liberties in humanising many of the animals that the narratives follow, which means some of their behaviour is not entirely accurate, despite the amount of research that went into each one, so you'll have to forgive me for that.

Another quick note is that "Whispering Walls" was previously included in the anthology *A Bridge of Shadow*, where it was titled "Shadow" and written under my pseudonym Kathryn Wells. I've included it here as I think the tone fits rather well with many of the other pieces.

Finally, I hope you enjoy reading this collection, and feel free to visit my website to find out about further works or email me with any questions you may have!

www.kathrynrossati.co.uk

A Tale Upon The Bard's Arrival

ONCE, there was a man whose tongue carried magic in every cell. It could weave webs from the simplest words and craft portraits straight from his imagination. But he had not always been a master of his powers.

You see, in his youth, his elders had thought his speech affected, and assigned him tutors and doctors to improve his diction and enouncement. Such was his level of study that his grasp of language rivalled that of most scholars. Yet what had caused this difficulty of speech was not an abnormal mouth nor laziness of wit, but the magic of his tongue itching to break free.

Years passed, and still his power was not allowed the freedom it sought, as the man had been told many times that his words, however clever, meant nothing. In their eyes, he was worthless. And without confidence to break its lock, his magic stayed trapped inside.

Then it happened that one day, when he'd all but given up hope that anyone could truly understand him, he met a woman who also possessed magic. Unlike him, she had already discovered her gift. It was quite different to his, for she could only express her magic through written words.

The man was fascinated by the woman's writings, enthralled by the wonder they brought forth. He itched to speak with her, and so, forgetting the hurt he'd been dealt by others, approached with a puzzle box containing a precious, rare ink. Twisting and turning it in the right combinations, he opened the box before her, presenting its prize.

With delight, she accepted his gift and together they spent a day talking of secrets neither thought they'd ever share with another person.

So at peace were they that the man's tongue finally allowed itself to free his magic. It spilled forth, vivid and beautiful, adding rainbows of colour to the surroundings and the fine ink within the pot.

The woman gave a joyful laugh. Seizing her quill, she dipped it into the pot and then wrote:

Sir, your words colour the landscape and make me warm. I feared the winters long chasing me had forever turned me to ice, but you have disproven that. How might I repay you?

The words shimmered as the ink dried, and grew into intricate flowers no bigger than a thumb.

The man smiled, plucking a flower and placing

it in her hair, saying, 'Let me befriend you so we may always be close. You've given me permission to be my truest self. No other has ever done so. *You* have aided *me*.'

Both knew they complemented each other, and though there were times when they had to travel apart, their hearts and minds were always one, and so it was that they worked together to keep wonder present in the world.

The Shades

MOLLY JUMPED out of her doze, disorientated for a moment by the shrill ring of the doorbell. It rang again, and this time she realised what it was. She glared at the grandmother clock on the wall. Five o'clock. *Who the devil is it? I'm not expecting anyone.*

She picked up her cane and heaved herself out of the armchair, managing to hobble over to the door. As she passed the window, she saw that a heavy gale was blowing and the snow had gotten deeper since last she'd looked. It was almost up to the wheel arches on her car.

She unlocked the door but, just as she turned the handle, the wind tore it open and knocked her backwards. It sent her sprawling to the floor, her cane rolling out of reach. Before she could get up, two figures darted through the doorway. One of them forced the door shut again and then knelt beside her, gently shaking her shoulder.

'Are you alright?'

Molly looked up. The voice was a woman's, and it was *very* familiar. 'Is it really you, Samantha?'

The figure removed her chequered scarf. 'Yes, Mother, it's me.'

Molly reached out a hand to touch her daughter's face, but recoiled at the last moment. 'Well, it's about time you showed up. My chimney is in dire need of sweeping.'

She took hold of the cupboard she was slumped against, and tried to ease herself up. Samantha grabbed her, taking most of her weight, but Molly shrugged her off and managed to pull herself upright. She stood breathing deeply and focused on the other figure in the room.

'Who on earth is that?'

'Calm down, Mother. This is Annie, and she is the reason I've come to see you.'

Molly looked at the girl huddled in the corner. She was so wrapped up in clothing that only her eyes were showing. They stared back at Molly, unblinking. *There is something wrong with this child.*

'How old are you, girl?' she asked. There was no reply, not even an acknowledgement that someone had spoken. Molly met her daughter's gaze. 'Well, you have my attention. I'll go and put the kettle on, and you can tell me all about it. Sit the child down in the lounge, it's much warmer in there.'

———

Molly and Samantha seated themselves around the wooden table in the kitchen, nursing cups of tea. Molly wrinkled her nose at the strong smell of polish. As always, she had used too much.

'Alright then, who is she? Where did you find her?' she asked crisply.

'She's an orphan. Her parents died in a fire about a year ago while she was on a school trip. She had no next of kin, but her neighbour kindly asked the court if she could look after her, and they agreed. The thing is, Annie hasn't spoken a word since then. I've been told she was a lively, bubbly girl who made friends easily and loved to paint and draw, but that's all fallen away now.'

'I was right not to have taken her silence personally, then,' Molly grunted, wrapping her thick woollen cardigan more tightly about her. 'How did you get involved?'

'I'm her neighbour's hairdresser. I do mobile work on the weekends, and so when I went there eight months ago, I met Annie. Each time Mrs Roberts had an appointment with me, she used to say she'd had someone round to try and get Annie to talk or take an interest in her hobbies again, but they were never successful.'

'So you brought her to me?'

'So I brought her to you.'

Molly took a long drink of tea, absently fingering a dent on the table. 'Well,' she said, putting the cup down, 'I don't think that this is a case of simply not wanting to talk, Samantha. I've seen that many times before, and this is different.'

'Different how?' Samantha asked.

'It seems to me that she's shut away her mind. She can follow simple commands, as I'm sure you know, but there is no emotional response. She's a robot, or at least she might as well be.'

Samantha's eyes grew troubled. 'Is there nothing you can do?'

'I'm not sure. If I can draw out her consciousness, then yes, but if my suspicions are correct, it will take more than my power to do so. She is an unusual child.' Molly drained her cup and picked up her cane again. 'Stay here, I need to talk to her alone.'

She got up and hobbled into the lounge where Annie was waiting. The girl was sitting close to the fire, staring into the flames. She had taken off her hat and coat, revealing long dark hair that fell down her back. *Just like mine when I was her age.*

'You'll burn your toes if you put them much closer,' Molly said, with a cluck of her tongue. There was no reaction. She sighed and sat back down in her chair, resting her cane back on the floor. *Now what? Perhaps …*

'I'm going to tell you a story, girl. You should listen,' she continued. 'Let's see now … where should I start? Back before civilisation began, on the vast barren plains of the continent, lived a small tribe. They had no home and no name, and wandered endlessly in search of food and water. For them, every day was a struggle, and often led to starvation and disease.

'Yet one day, a particularly violent storm hit the area, and with it came a fierce earthquake that split the ground in two. From the chasm that formed, a green vapour spilled out and encompassed the tribe. It put them into a deep slumber for many days, and some of the elders died through lack of nourishment, but when the tribe finally awoke, they found that the vapour had solidified into shards of emerald crystal. As soon as they touched it, every one of their senses became heightened. They could hear the thoughts of those around them, and conversed telepathically. Their lives now had a new meaning, and a new purpose. Using their powers, they gathered information from the other tribes around them on where to find sources of food and water. No longer did they have to wander desperately on the brink of starvation.

'For many years they prospered, and their abilities continued to develop. Soon they could even shut off part of a person's mind to prevent them from remembering the tribe's location or spread rumours of their powers, and it was found that children born to the tribe from then on also had those abilities. Even so, they could not keep themselves a secret from the other tribes forever. They became known as Shades—evil spirits—and the other tribes feared that not only would they leach every food source from them, but their very lives as well. They decided to take action against the Shades, and so joined forces to mount an attack. Hundreds were killed, but a handful of children managed to escape. Those children were my ancestors, Annie, and I too have the same powers as they, though mine are far weaker.'

Annie hadn't moved throughout the story, but Molly knew it had reached her. She had been projecting images into the girl's mind as she was speaking, and there had been little resistance.

'Turn around, child.'

Annie turned as Molly knew she would. Her eyes were still unfocused, but there was something —a glimmer of hope, perhaps? *I can feel her mind. It's almost as though it's encased in a shell. If I can break that, then surely I can return her to normal.*

'Another child would question that tale and say that it isn't possible for a mind to gain so much power at the touch of a crystal. They would say that it is the content of fairy tales, not real life. You, however, do not question. Like the Shades discovered, you know that it is possible to close the mind, and you dare to hope that it can be awakened once again.'

Annie blinked. Molly fought hard not to smile. It was only a small response, but it was a response none-the-less. *Her mind is stirring, but not enough. She is too strong for me to release her. There is only one way.*

Yet it was late now, and the effort had drained much of Molly's strength. She was sure Annie needed rest, too. She got up once again and hobbled out into the kitchen where Samantha was waiting. As she left, she saw Annie turn back to the fire, moving her toes away ever so slightly.

'The girl needs sleep. Show her to the guestroom.'

Samantha, who had just opened her mouth to speak, shut it again hastily and obliged without question. The stairs creaked as she and Annie made their way to the bedroom.

Molly had seen many people drawn in by their grief, but not to the extent that Annie was. *But no one else had that kind of strength, and there's only one reason for a girl her age to possess it.*

The stairs creaked again, and Samantha returned. She looked worn and stretched, as though she hadn't had much rest lately herself. 'Did you get her to speak?' she asked.

'No. It is beyond my own abilities to help her,' Molly replied.

'So there's no hope?' Samantha said despondently. 'I thought for sure—'

'I didn't say that. It's true I can't do it myself, but there *is* a way.'

For a moment, Samantha was confused. Then her eyes widened. 'You … you mean to use the shard?'

'Yes.'

'But that could kill her!'

'Indeed it could, but I strongly suspect it won't. If she were a normal child then I wouldn't dare use it, but then if she were a normal child I wouldn't have to. You must have felt it, just as I did. I suspect that's what drew you to her in the first place.'

'Perhaps I felt something, yes, but what are you suggesting?'

'That she is Shade, just as we are.'

'Shade? Are you sure?'

'Of course I'm sure,' Molly snapped. 'That is why only the shard can draw her out again. However, once it is done, she will be a fully awakened Shade, just as the first ones were. She will need guidance and proper training. We'll have no choice but to keep her here.'

'But Mrs Roberts—'

'Will have to give up custody of her. You've always had a way with people, I'm sure you can convince her, and the courts too, if necessary.'

———

It was early, but Molly was already up and fully clothed. Heading down to the kitchen and out the back door, she made her way to the stone shed at the bottom of the garden. She didn't bother waking Samantha; it would do her good to lie in.

The snow was still deep and the wind seemed to eat away at Molly's bones. Thankfully, the lock on the shed door wasn't frozen and opened easily. She slipped inside, glad of the slight warmth. The light flickered as she pulled the switch, finally settling into a dull glow, just enough to see by.

There was a cupboard in the middle of the floor, and Molly cursed when she saw it. *You old fool, how could you have forgotten that was there?* Putting down her cane, she took the sides of the cupboard and pushed with what little strength she had.

The cupboard moved, but slowly. Molly's tired limbs were not what they once were, and she had to stop after each push to catch her breath. Eventually, she eased it off the loose floorboard she was after and, with much grunting, lowered herself to the floor. She lifted up the floorboard, revealing a hole where an old chest lay, covered in dust. Producing a polished brass key from her pocket, she opened it.

Inside was a bundle of wrapped silk. She picked it up, making sure the silk was still firmly bound around the object inside. Her body tingled as energy radiated out of it to replenish her stamina, and refreshed, she made her way back to the house.

When she opened the kitchen door, Annie was sitting at the table. She didn't look up as Molly walked in, but shifted slightly in her seat. *Can she sense the shard's power?*

Samantha appeared from the hall in her dressing gown, looking very apprehensive. She stared at the silk bundle Molly still held, and her lip trembled.

'Is that …?' she asked.

'Yes,' Molly said, setting it down on the table. 'Is she well rested?'

'Yes, she didn't wake until I called on her five minutes ago.'

'Good. It's time,' Molly said. She turned to Annie. 'Do you remember the story I told you last night, child? About the tribe who touched the crystal shards and had their minds awakened?'

Annie looked up from her tea cup, and slowly shifted her gaze to the silk bundle.

'Inside that bundle is one of those very shards. It will help you if you touch it.'

This time Annie moved her hand forward slightly in the direction of the bundle. It was all Molly needed to be sure. She found the knot on the silk and undid it, carefully unwinding the cloth until the slim green shard was visible. She daren't touch the bare crystal herself, to expose her aged body to such a jolt of power would damage her mind beyond repair.

Samantha took hold of one of Annie's hands and laid it flat on the table. Ever so gently, Molly let the shard touch it. Annie gave a shudder and fainted. Molly quickly took the shard away and wrapped it up once more.

'Do you think it worked?' Samantha whispered.

'Yes. We must take her to her room and let her recover.'

─────

An urgent knocking woke Molly from her sleep.

'What is it?' she shouted, fumbling with the covers.

'She's awake, mother, she's awake!'

Molly stumbled over to the door, ignoring her aching back, and opened it. Samantha was standing before her, her hair tumbling haphazardly across her face. 'Well, of course she's awake,' Molly said curtly. 'Has she spoken yet?'

'No, not yet.'

'Take me to her, then.'

When they arrived in Annie's room, she was sitting at the head of the bed with her knees tucked up against her chin. Her eyes were wild, as though she'd just woken from a nightmare. Molly could feel her mind writhing, trying to make sense of what it now felt.

'Tell me your name, child,' she said, pushing past her daughter and sitting on the end of the bed.

'A … An … Annie.'

Behind Molly, Samantha gasped. 'It worked! It *really* worked.'

'Samantha, be quiet. We need to keep her calm,' Molly shushed.

'Where … where am I?' Annie asked.

'This is Shady Lake House, child. It has been my home for many years, and now it will be your home, too. I'm sure you have many questions that I will gladly answer, but first I think you could do with a nice strong cup of tea.'

Annie put her knees down and turned to sit with her legs dangling off the bed. She looked at Molly. 'Do you have any biscuits?'

Molly chuckled, a cackling, boiling-pot of a laugh that made Annie draw back. 'Yes, child, we have plenty of biscuits.'

Merry Weather

AT FIRST, I didn't see her. She was caught between two bushes, tangled in cobwebs, spindly branches and the lacy trim of her silvery blue cape. I did hear her, though. Cursing so much that I thought a group of drunken sailors had strolled around the corner from the pub in town.

But no. All the swearing was emanating from a tiny fairy, red in the face from her efforts to untangle herself.

If it wasn't for the fact that she saw me and gave such a scowl that my legs automatically wanted to run for the hills, I might have laughed. Instead, I mumbled an offer of assistance while pulling my most solemn expression, and stepped forwards to help.

My fingers slipped in my attempt to de-cobweb her and I ended up jabbing her in the head. She bit me for that. Straight through the skin, so that a bead of blood rose from the puncture wound and stained her clothes. I murmured concern, but her long frenzy of expletives detailing every inch of my incompetence drowned it out. Then she wept, equally as loudly, about the state of her clothes and how they were positively *ruined.*

I think it was supposed to make me feel sorry for her, but in actuality it made her terrifying hold on me weaken enough to simply pinch her roughly out of the tangled mess, tearing her cloak completely. She wailed even more. I bluntly pointed out that she was free and if she hadn't been wearing the ridiculous thing, she probably wouldn't have ended up in that state in the first place.

In answer, she took a small stick from the top of one boot and jabbed it at my nose. Hot sparks shot out the end, singeing my nostril hairs. I let her go in disgust and watched her zoom away, emitting the wettest raspberry I'd ever heard. At least, I *hope* it was a raspberry ....

Whispering Walls

ESH PACED across the wooden decking, lit by the moon's brightness, still holding the letter in his hands that had summoned him there. Brief words, with no signature: the usual style, though it was true he hadn't received one in some time.

The dockside was empty, the sailors already bedded down for the night, or otherwise occupied elsewhere. The only thing near was his shadow and the only sounds the lapping of inky waves against rotting, weed-encrusted deck boards and the far-off hum of tavern patrons singing in their drunken stupors.

Kivuli watched his master, listening to every step he took, knowing that soon someone would join them. Malkov. Kivuli's dark form paled slightly at the thought, for Malkov was a man who commanded complete obedience, an obedience that his master, against his better judgement, found impossible not to give.

A second set of footsteps sounded in the night. Esh stopped his pacing. A figure was approaching, walking erect and with purpose. As the light hit him, Kivuli saw his face. Strong cheekbones jutted on either side, and his hair was long and straight, framing eyes so bright that they seemed to burn with an inner fire. A perfectly trimmed goatee sprang from his chin and, despite the warmth of the night, he wore a thick cloak and held a polished black walking cane at his side. He stopped in front of Esh, who bowed low before him, licking his dry lips. 'You have a task for me, my Lord?' Esh asked, his tone hushed.

Malkov said nothing. Instead he looked around, and his bright eyes locked on Kivuli for the faintest of seconds, boring down on him as if he knew that the shadow was more than a grey form on the floor. He turned back to Esh. 'You were not followed?'

'Of course not, my Lord,' Esh replied. 'My methods are not so lax, even if it has been some time since I last had need of them.'

'Good. I was afraid you might have become …
rusty … over the years. You know your skills have served me well in the past. I must call on them again.'

Kivuli stretched away from Esh, unable to stand Malkov's terrible presence. He suddenly felt someone beside him and jumped back, merging with the shadows of the docks.

'Calm yourself, Kivuli, it is only I,' a voice said next to him.

Kivuli recognised it. It was the same as Malkov's, but there was no hint of hardness in it. 'Ombra?' he asked.

'Indeed. Surely you were expecting me? After all, is it not *my* master with whom yours now speaks?'

'I—it didn't occur to me,' Kivuli replied. 'You know how your master makes me feel. I can't concentrate on anything when he's near.'

Ombra gave a low chuckle. 'You should take comfort then, Kivuli, for there are many who fear him. There are times when even I tremble in his presence.'

'Truly? You're afraid of your own master?'

'He is cruel and ruthless. If he does not get what he wants, his anger is unquenchable. It would be folly not to fear him.'

'But what *does* he want? My master's carried out tasks for him twice now, and both times he came across danger. If this new request is anything like those, then I can't bear to think of what might happen to him. I've got to help him, Ombra, for his own sake,' Kivuli said solemnly.

'No.'

It was one word, but it struck Kivuli silent.

'You know our laws, Kivuli. You must never reveal yourself to him. *Never* let the humans know what we are capable of. Only a fool would think of exposing us.'

Without a word more, Ombra slid away to his master, who now turned away from Esh and strode back into the darkness of the night. Esh stayed for a while, watching the tide swell in and out, but eventually grew tired. With Kivuli behind him, they made their way to the squalid streets of town.

Half-clad women called out to Esh as he travelled the back alleys, keen to stay away from more reputable eyes, flashing what little skin was still covered by their threadbare clothes. Kivuli knew Esh had no taste for their unwashed lips tonight, not now he had a job to do. Besides, even the times when he did share their company, Kivuli couldn't help but feel it was only his master's way of suppressing the thoughts that forever haunted him.

They took their usual winding path to Esh's home, which, so far, not even the most skilled pickpockets and spies had managed to follow. They exited by a rotten staircase that jutted out into a minor street. Esh darted up it and unlocked the door at the top.

It was black inside, but he struck a match and lit an oil lamp just inside the door. It revealed the narrow corridor they were in, leading to a single door. Inside, the room was small, with a straw mattress at one end, and a crude wooden desk and chair at the other. A fireplace was set into the back wall, while a basin stood in the corner, with a jug of clean water and a cloth resting on the side. Papers littered the floor. Most of them were sketches of people Esh had been commissioned to track at one time or another, others were old journals and childish scribblings once belonging to his wife and daughter, lost so many years ago from a plague when they'd crossed the sea to the mainland with the hope of living a more prosperous life.

Kivuli missed their shadows, how they had laughed and played and grown together. *His* family. It was seven years that moon since they'd been lost, their life extinguished along with their masters'. He and Esh had been immune. Watching them die was one thing neither of them would ever forget, no matter how much they wished to.

Esh picked up one of his daughter's scribblings, tracing the ink marks with his fingertips before letting it drop from his grasp to drift back to the floor. He slumped in the chair, his head dropping to rest on the rough grain of the desk. Kivuli looked on from where he stood against the wall, blending in with the darkness of the room, wishing that he was more than a shadow, wishing he could break the laws binding him so he could help his master. Whatever Malkov had planned for Esh, it wasn't good. Kivuli knew it, down in his very being. He had to do *something*.

———

The sun had risen high before Kivuli saw his master begin to stir. Realising how late it was, Esh jumped up, knocking over the desk he'd fallen asleep at. He splashed some water on his face, running a hand through his hair, and put on a clean cotton tunic, woollen jacket and trousers.

Throwing one last glance at the scattered papers, which Kivuli lingered by in the light, he strode from the room, down the corridor, and out into the morning air, already stagnant with the reek of soiled foods, sweat and seaweed.

They headed to a run-down tavern in the centre of town, far from Esh's usual place to meet clients. The smell of spilled ale and stale vomit emanating from the straw-covered floor made Esh's brow sweat. Kivuli looked around at the other customers, and noticed that both men and shadow alike had an unsavoury aura. Shaking a little, he stayed close to his master, who had chosen to sit in the corner, as far away from them as he could get.

A serving girl, little more than a child, came over to see what Esh wanted. She wore a dress so patched and filthy that it was hard to tell what the original colour might have been. Kivuli caught several eyes ogling her from across the room. He shuddered, noticing Esh do the same. The girl was only a few years older than his daughter had been when she'd died. For her to be working in a place like this …

'Ale,' Esh answered to her unasked question. She nodded and went to fetch it.

As she came back, spilling most of it on the floor as rowdy patrons jostled and knocked against her, Kivuli saw a man walk in wearing a rough-spun cloak. The hood concealed most of his face, but on seeing Esh he lowered it to reveal an angular jaw and a nose that had the tell-tale slant of having been broken at some point. He walked over, grinning as though meeting an old friend, but Kivuli was sure his master had never met him before. He looked around for the man's shadow, and saw it just a little way away from him. It too was angular, and Kivuli didn't recognise it.

'Fancy seein' you 'ere, friend,' the man said, sitting down at the table next to Esh. His voice was slurred, with a dryness to it that Kivuli didn't like. Then he put his hands on the table and interlaced his fingers, dropping both index fingers quickly and then pointing them up again.

Esh swallowed and hitched up one of his sleeves just long enough to reveal three silvery scars, slashed through with a fourth. Malkov's mark, received six years ago as a reward for surviving the first task he'd been set. The man grunted and drew a small bundle from inside his cloak, passing it to Esh under the table. Kivuli moved closer to look at it, but the man's shadow clawed at him with a hiss. He drew back quickly, just as the man got up again.

'Sorry ta leave ya already, friend,' he said. 'Tho

I 'spect we'll be seein' each other soon enuff.' He turned away, hiding his face under his hood once more, and left the tavern. Esh and Kivuli watched him leave, but no one else spared him a second glance.

Five minutes later, Esh downed his ale and left a coin on the table for the serving girl to collect, before leaving himself.

———

Back in their room, Esh opened the bundle. Inside was a bag containing a strange powder and a scrap of paper. Putting the powder aside, he unfolded the paper and read, mumbling the words loud enough for Kivuli to hear. 'Ignite the powder when all is done. Do not ready it until the switch has been made. Do not dally, we shall be watching.' He inhaled deeply and scrunched the paper in his hand, throwing it against the wall. It bounced off and landed on top of one of his wife's journals.

Seeing it, his eyes suddenly turned watery, and he sank to his knees, putting his head in his hands. 'Please, Maggie,' he sobbed, tears dripping through his fingers. 'Please … don't judge me too much …'

His sobbing went on until Kivuli was sure there were no more tears left for his master to shed. Then, with a look of crazed anger, Esh smashed his fist against the floor. Gathering up the journals, he threw them onto the hearth and took a match from his pocket, ready to strike it.

'Stop!'

Esh froze, the match hovering inches from the friction paper. 'Who … who said that? Is someone there?' He wiped his face roughly on his sleeve, pocketing the match again, and went over to the door, thrusting it open to stare down the corridor. When he saw no one there, he went back to the fireplace. Kivuli tried to keep silent, but then his master struck the match.

'No, master, please!'

Kivuli couldn't stop himself. His master was a good man, he didn't deserve to be dragged down by the likes of Malkov and his men.

'Who's there?' Esh said again, his skin paling.

Kivuli shook slightly, but he had made his choice. Speaking to one's master was forbidden, no matter what the circumstance, but Esh was too important for him to care. 'Master, please. Look at the wall next to you,' Kivuli instructed. In the light coming from the window, his outline was distinct against the wall. His master looked at him, still uncomprehending. 'Master, I am your shadow.'

Silence. Esh didn't move or waver so much as an inch, despite the match burning down to his fingertips. He just stood, staring at Kivuli, his expression unchanged. At last he spoke, wetting his lips with his tongue. 'My shadow?' He walked closer to the wall and held out his hand, touching Kivuli lightly as though he might suddenly attack.

'Yes, master,' Kivuli whispered. He lifted his arm independently, with deliberate slowness so as not to cause more alarm. His master's eyes followed it, growing wide and glistening slightly.

'No. This isn't real. Just a trick of the light, that's all. Or there was something in that ale. You can't move on your own, and you certainly can't talk on your own either.'

'Please Master, I understand that this is a shock, but you *must* listen.'

Esh drew his lips tight and shook his head.

Kivuli sighed. He walked around the room, moving from wall to wall and across the floor, merging with the static shadows and then reappearing again. 'You see?' he asked.

Esh had seen. He grabbed for the wooden chair and sat down heavily, still watching Kivuli with a wild look in his eyes. 'How …?' he breathed.

'That doesn't matter. Please, you must reconsider your involvement with Malkov.'

'Malkov?' Esh blinked. 'I'd forgotten.'

'Master, I've spoken with Malkov's shadow—'

'His shadow can speak too?'

'All shadows belonging to living creatures can speak,' Kivuli said softly. 'Those that can speak the human tongue, at least. Malkov's shadow is called Ombra, and even he fears him. I have no doubt that Malkov thinks of you as expendable.'

Esh stood up and picked up a dusty wineskin from under the straw mattress. He opened it and took a long drink, wiping his mouth after. He took a few steps away from Kivuli, but then turned back to him. 'I know that Malkov's using me. And I know he's dangerous. But tell me, shadow of mine, what is it I'm supposed to do? If I survive this job, I'll earn enough money to go back home and escape this place … and leave my pain behind. And if I back out now, he'll only hunt me down.'

'Then go to him first.'

Esh laughed. A desperate, pitying sound. 'That would be suicide.'

'Not necessarily. Malkov is a man who expects to get what he wants. If you hold your ground, you'll surprise him. He might just let you go.'

'He might … or he might not.' Esh paced around some more. 'Damn it! Alright, shadow, have it your way. I'm probably dead anyway.'

———

Kivuli and Esh watched Malkov's house from where they sat in wait in the tavern opposite, in the rich quarter of town. It was the evening Esh was to carry out Malkov's plans, and they knew that soon the rest of Malkov's men would be leaving to set up everything. Malkov himself would be alone.

Two hours passed before the grand doors of the house opened, and five men came out, making their way down the street. With a slight tremor, Kivuli noticed the man Esh had met at the other tavern, hovering at the back of the group, with his shadow snapping at its fellows.

Waiting until they turned the corner and disappeared from sight, Kivuli and Esh left the relative safety of the tavern and went outside to Malkov's house. Following Kivuli's plan to surprise him, they avoided the main door and went around to the side, where they knew the entrance to the cellars was. Esh had been marked down there. It wasn't a memory easily erased.

When they reached it, they found the gate locked and chained—no more than they'd expected. Esh took out a thin knife and a stolen hairpin to try and pick it open. To help him, Kivuli slid his hand into the lock and told him which way it needed to be turned. A moment later, it clicked open, and they descended into the cellar.

The void inside hit them sharply, and for a moment Kivuli was lost in it. Searching around the wooden crates and barrels stored around them, he felt about until his dark hands brushed lumps of melted wax. Tracing it upwards, his fingers closed around the stump of a candle with just enough of a wick in it to light. He rolled it over to Esh, where it bumped against his boots. Esh lit it immediately, and filled the room with a warm, flickering glow. With the staircase to the main house now illuminated, they went up, coming out into the hall.

There they paused, hiding behind a large, marble bust on a pedestal, listening for any signs of Malkov.

Loud voices sounded from a room further down, and a manservant came running from it, holding a blood-soaked cloth to his arm. Kivuli and Esh shrank back as he passed, but then edged down the hall to peer through the door.

'I should have had a report back by now,' they heard Malkov say. 'Something is wrong. Even from here, we should have heard an explosion.' He sounded panicked, and the dominance had completely disappeared from his voice.

'You fret much, Malkov. All shall go to plan.'

'But you said his shadow was concerned. What if he suspected we were setting Esh up to be framed for it. If he talked him out—'

'Kivuli does not possess the courage to break the Laws of Shadow. A simple word from myself kept those thoughts of his at bay. He would never reveal himself to Esh.' It was Ombra speaking.

Before he knew what he was doing, Kivuli had slipped into the room. There they were. Malkov, sitting in a fur-backed chair near the fire, his eyes now dull and his goatee untrimmed. Ombra was on the wall next to him, stretched out to his largest form, distorted so much that he barely resembled Malkov at all.

'Ombra?' Kivuli murmured.

Malkov sat up, startled by the soft voice. He

looked around, and his eyes locked on Esh, as he, too, stepped inside the room. 'You!' he exclaimed, half-standing, but Ombra silenced him.

'It seems I have made a grave error, Kivuli. You are obviously not the coward I took you for. To think you broke our laws so easily! I have to say, I am somewhat impressed. You, however,' he said, rounding on Malkov, who seemed to melt into his chair; every sign of the confident tyrant they'd taken him to be gone from his composure. 'You *assured* me that this scoundrel of a man would be too fearful to back out.'

'Ombra, this was all you?' Kivuli asked, the disbelief only too clear in his voice. 'Why?'

'How many thousands of years have we shadows been but mere attachments, shackled to these buffoons but never able act upon our own will? Silenced for fear of alarming them?' Ombra hissed. 'Well, I say no more. It is time for change, Kivuli. Humans are weak and filled with greed and hatred; we can let ourselves be ruled by them no longer. *We* must strive to be the masters now.' He slid over to Malkov, who withdrew even more. 'It is a sad thing that my life is forever tied to yours,' he whispered. 'If it were not so, I would have killed you long ago. As it is, I must instead command you to dispose of these two fools. Hesitate, and I shall do so myself. You will find the sight *far* less pleasant.'

Malkov got up shakily and drew a rapier from

its display on the wall above the fireplace. Despite being used as an ornament, Kivuli could see the point was still sharp. He glanced at Malkov's face. The man's eyes had grown glassy; his heart was not in it. Still, Kivuli couldn't see a way to stop him, and with Ombra controlling him, words were useless. He looked at his master, who stood still despite Malkov's advancement. He caught a slight bulge in Esh's jacket pocket.

Suddenly, he *knew*.

He swept up and whispered something in Esh's ear, speaking quickly.

'But what'll happen to you?' Esh whispered back.

'Don't worry, master. Please, you have no time!'

'Then at least tell me your name, shadow. I haven't even asked,' Esh said urgently.

'It's Kivuli.'

With a quick nod, Esh dipped his hand into his jacket pocket, withdrawing the powder that had been in the bundle. As Malkov readied his rapier to strike, Esh charged him, ducking under his sword arm and driving him back into Ombra with as much force as he could muster. Then he threw the powder into the fire beside them. The flames leapt up, birthing forth a brilliant, blinding light, engulfing them all.

It hit Ombra full on. The shadow let out a roar of undiluted agony, then dissolved into nothingness.

———

The effects of the powder finally dulled, but it was an hour before both Malkov and Esh had recovered their sight. When they were at last able to look around, they found both Kivuli and Ombra missing.

'Have they both … gone?' Malkov asked, searching the whole room. Only static shadows surrounded them.

'I think so,' Esh answered with a remorseful sigh.

'Why so solemn, master?' Kivuli's voice sounded faintly amused. 'Could it be that you felt a loss for me?'

'Kivuli? Where are you?' Esh asked.

'Open your jacket, master.'

Esh did so, and Kivuli's grey form poured out of it and onto the floor.

'And Ombra?' Malkov breathed.

'He is *truly* gone,' Kivuli replied. 'There was no chance for him to hide as I did. You are a free man, now. Though,' he added, snaking over to him, 'I have one request for you. Release my master from your service and fund his journey home. We've both had more than our share of horrors in this place.'

Insight

WE WATCHED him unpack the leather-bound boxes, producing all manner of strange objects: hats, scarves, candles, and parts of some complicated contraption. Already a crowd had started to gather, ladies, gentlemen and even children, though he was obviously far from ready. He had no assistant to help, nor, I believe, did he need one.

Each object, no matter how seemingly unimportant, paid he the utmost attention, and placed it so precisely, only a master of his art could he be.

With everything set as he would wish, and with the crowd so large that several shoppers in the square had begun to complain, he stood before us, dressed in top hat and tailcoat, his gloved hands raised to command attention.

'Ladies and gentlemen,' said he, his voice rich and sonorous. 'Today, you shall bear witness to wonders you have never before seen. Today, you will question truth, logic and even yourselves.'

We could not help but be drawn in by his speech, and as he calmly demonstrated his abilities, starting with the levitation of a glass orb, followed by the sudden vanishing of an ornately carved cabinet, we admitted that we were indeed witnessing wonders.

'And now, ladies and gentlemen, I require a volunteer. Ah, yes, madam, if you would please step forward. Yes, yes, here we are now.'

Astonished as we were, we found ourselves stepping forward and, after he had placed a cushioned chair before us, we sat in front of the crowd, awaiting the master's instructions. Up close, we could see that his white collar was somewhat stained, his jacket far from clean. Yet his eyes were still sharp, bright and inspecting us with rapt attention.

He held out a pocket watch, instructing us to follow its movement as it swung from side to side. We felt our eyes grow heavy and faintly heard the master speak again, though now he sounded far away, all but an echo in our ears. Our eyes closed fully and a fog, thick but somehow light, filled our heads.

For how long we stayed in that state, we do not know, but eventually the master spoke again. We could not comprehend what he said, but we understood his meaning. The fog drifted away, and we felt as though wings had sprouted from our shoulders and were lifting us to the skies.

'Now open your eyes.'

Our eyes opened.

No, *my* eyes opened.

'You alright there, love? Gave me an' the boys a right nasty scare, seeing you collapse the way you did.' The middle-aged man standing over me smelt of liquor and sweat, but seemed genuinely concerned. Two more men stood behind him, staring at me pityingly.

'I collapsed? But what happened to the magician?'

He gave me a confused look and helped me sit up. People were rushing through the Piazza, going in and out of shops, sparing not a glance at us. In the distance, car horns screeched at one other as cabbies stopped at the behest of their passengers. I knew this place and yet it was entirely foreign. It was not the Covent Garden I'd been in moments before. And nowhere, no matter which way I looked, could I see the magician.

I stood up, gingerly testing my balance, and thanked the gents for stopping to help me.

'You should see a doctor really, love,' the man who'd spoken before advised.

I mumbled a reply and waved as they walked away, glancing back a few times to check on me. As they disappeared into the tide, I put my hand in my pocket. My fingers touched something cool and circular. I drew the object out to examine it.

My breath caught.

I held the very pocket watch that was the last thing I'd seen before my world was shaken upside down. A name was engraved on the back, inside the symbol of an ace of spades.

Of course. It was my father's watch, and I'd planned on pawning it off.

A New Family

HYDA HELD her mother closely for the last time. Now she was of age, she must leave her family and find another in order to continue her genetic line. Her brothers, however, were to stay with their mother and wait for females from outside groups to find them.

Watching their sister leave and waiting for strangers to arrive left them apprehensive. If they didn't get along with one another, there was no chance of strengthening the family group.

Hyda only hoped that the new family she joined would accept her as their own, and as was custom, that she would find a mate she truly liked.

Staying high in the trees, her ears twitched to track the calls of the other spider monkeys living nearby. Unlike her family, who were white-bellied spider monkeys, these other groups were not. It would take many days of travel to find others of her kind. She knew there must be some, for last year two females had joined her family from two separate groups. They'd told her the journey was long, and Hyda had noted their words.

Reaching out to take hold of a branch, she swung, letting go at the top of her arc to fall a short way and then gracefully catch a branch from the next tree on her path.

It was odd moving through the trees without her brothers, but there was another feeling rising inside her. Excitement. For the first time in her life, she could go anywhere and do anything she wanted—until she found herself another group to join. But for now, she planned to enjoy her freedom.

She continued for another half day, using both her arms and tail to guide her through the great web of branches. After a while, her throat began to grow parched and there were no wet fruits around to take her thirst away. Below her was a large stretch of water sparkling in the late afternoon sun.

Searching with her eyes to make sure there were no predators in her immediate vicinity, she dropped down the branches, one by one, until she was on the lowest, stretching out across the water.

Wrapping her tail firmly around the branch, she lowered herself down. Stretching out Searching with her eyes to her hands to gather up the cool liquid, she brought them to her mouth and drank deeply. The water was sweet and didn't quite satisfy her thirst, so she took another handful and was about to take one more, when the fur on her back began to tingle. She looked around and was just in time to see two large eyes peering at her from the water's surface, with a long pointed snout directly beneath her.

As the creature snapped, she managed to swing out of its way, grabbing the branch with her hands and scrambling back up to the top of the tree. The creature, disappointed, sank back below the water and she watched its shadow as it swam downstream. She clung to the tree, her heart still dancing about in her chest. How could she have been so stupid? Her mother had warned her of creatures like that, and she even had a vague memory of watching another mammal being snatched away with those great jaws.

A chatter of harsh laughter rang out across the canopy and Hyda saw a whole group of monkeys observing her from the opposite side of the river. They were laughing so hard that some of them lost their balance and fell off the branch, dangling by their tails.

'Stupid white belly!' they called. 'Maybe you should play in the river some more!'

In disgust, she howled and bared her teeth. They laughed even more so, her temper rising, she swung off before it overtook her. She was a lone female, and a small one for her age at that. There was nothing she could do against such a large group.

She passed another group of monkeys, but still they weren't the other white bellies she sought. Yet they weren't aggressive towards her, contenting themselves to watch her pass without interruption, except to point her in the direction of a tree full of fruits, which she gathered and ate gladly.

The night drew in quickly after that, so climbing to the very top of the canopy to scout for predators, she wrapped her tail around a strong upright branch and curled her legs up to her chest, resting against the trunk.

Her eyes closed, but she did not sleep straight away. Instead, she listened; bats and large owls soared through the air and other nocturnal creatures howled as they hunted. Nothing approached her, however, so at last she deemed it safe drift off.

———

The sunlight hit her eyes the next morning, but as she raised her head, she jumped up in surprise, almost falling from the branch.

Two bright eyes stared at her, and as she looked back, she saw an orange triangle on the creature's forehead, with a mass of black fur covering the rest of its head along with its back, legs and tail. A creamy orange patch adorned its stomach.

Another white-bellied spider monkey!

'You're like me,' she said, unsure what a male was doing out here. She looked around, but couldn't see any signs of his group anywhere. 'Where are the others?'

'Others? Oh, you mean my family group?' he asked. She nodded. He shrugged. 'I don't have one.'

'What do you mean? You must have one.'

He shook his head. 'No, it's just me. Well, it was, but now I've found you. So I guess it's just us.' She frowned, so he continued. 'I was stolen from my group as a baby by some humans. They put me in a cage and were taking me somewhere away from the forest, but something happened and the cage was damaged. I ran away from them, but my leg was cut and so they trapped me again. But they were different humans this time. These ones helped me and fixed my leg. And gave me food. I've been living around here ever since.'

'Wait,' Hyda said, trying to absorb everything he'd blurted. 'What are these *humans* you talk about? And did you never try to find your own kind?'

'Humans are strange creatures. They're like hairless versions of us, except that they live on the ground and have no tails. Some of them are dangerous, but others aren't so bad. The ones who saved me live not far from here and if I can't find any food, I go down to them and they feed me. Sometimes there are strangers among them, but they never hurt me like the others did. That's why I've never looked for my group. I've never needed to.'

Hyda examined him closely. He was older than

her, but not by much, and he had a carelessness about him that she had never seen before in a male of her species. Still, these human creatures sounded suspicious, and if he relied on them despite what they'd done to him, that made *him* suspicious too.

'What's your name?' she asked, unwrapping her tail from the branch and curling it around herself.

'Kido,' he said. 'What's yours?'

'It's Hyda,' she said. 'And I'm afraid I must go now.'

'Go where?' he asked, his eyes going wide.

Was he concerned for her? 'I've got to find another group. It's tradition that when we females come of age, we leave our families and find new ones,' she said matter-of-factly.

'That sounds horrible. If I'd grown up knowing my family, I don't think I would want to leave them like that,' he said, a visible tremor running through him.

She laughed. 'You wouldn't have to. The males stay and wait for new females to join from other groups. My brothers still live in the same group as my mother and are waiting even now for the new females to arrive.'

Kido frowned. 'I've got a better idea,' he said, and grabbed her hand, leading her from tree to tree. They rushed through the treetops so fast she could barely take in any of her surroundings.

Why had this naïve male dragged her off so suddenly? She had to find a new family soon or else she would be left on her own—or worse—with this fool.

'Where are you taking me? I demand that you tell me!' she screamed as he jumped from the top branches of one tree to cascade down to the bottom of another.

She fell along with him, unable to break free of his grip, her stomach jumping up to her throat as she realised she would have to rely on him to get a strong hold on the next branch so that their con-joined weight wouldn't make his hand slip and send them plunging into the water.

As he landed his grip however, she realised there had been nothing to fear. Kido's body was so accus-tomed to making leaps from such heights that having more weight and the use of just one hand didn't even tire him as he held on to the sturdy branch. He swung upwards and planted his feet on it, finally releasing his hold on her.

'I'm taking you to where the humans are,' he said, pausing for a moment.

'Why? I need to find a family to join, not run around with you and be a plaything for those crea-tures. What if they turn out to be bad, like the ones who took you from your home as a baby?' she said, unsure whether to laugh at him or bare her teeth.

'They're not like that. Not at all. It sometimes feels as though *they* are my family, even the ones who seem to be different at each visit.' He stood up and held out his hand. 'Let me show you.'

The sun had moved past its highest point by then, and she was hungry. She hesitated, then reluctantly took it. 'If you really wish me to see them, I'll go. But I won't stay. I cannot.'

'I understand,' he said, and they took off through the trees again.

———

As the sun neared its final arc, Kido and Hyda reached what looked like a giant swollen node resting between two tree trunks. There was a hole in it where flat ground-that-was-not-ground stretched out towards them. It was filled with creatures resembling furless monkeys, except they had no tails, and judging by the awkward rigidity of their backs and limbs, were unsuited to climbing through the trees. They also seemed to be covered in large, intricate types of leaves that Hyda had never come across before, presumably to hide their bare skin.

'What are those things?' she asked Kido quietly, in case the creatures spotted her.

'Those are the humans,' he said. 'Come, if we show ourselves, they'll feed us.'

He swung across to land in the branches just in front of the ground-that-was-not-ground. 'Look,' one of the humans said loudly, pointing. 'It's a white-bellied spider monkey!' The rest of the humans turned and chattered excitedly. The fur on Hyda's back bristled.

Another human came up to look, gently pushing through the crowd. 'Oh, yes, that's Kido. He's one of our regulars. I expect he's come here for his dinner,' it said.

This one's voice was slightly higher, and Hyda had a strong instinctual feeling that it was female. Suddenly, it glanced up in her direction and gasped. 'Well, well, Kido,' it said, smiling. 'Have you finally found a mate, I wonder?'

The female human walked off for a moment, but when it came back, it had a large bundle of fruits in its arms. She threw one to Kido, who caught it easily and began to eat. Then it held one out for Hyda, calling to her.

At first, Hyda refused to move, watching the humans babble as Kido ate, and throw him more as soon as he'd finished. They made no move to capture him, despite being close enough to do so.

Eventually, her hunger grew so strong she began to climb down to them, but remained on guard.

Nothing happened, so she took a spot next to Kido and caught one of the fruits that the female threw to her. She bit into it, feeling the juice run down the fur of her chin. It was sweet and fleshy.

'Is this one a regular too?' the first human who'd spoken asked.

The female shook its head. 'I've never seen this one before. She looks fairly young though, so I presume she's out looking for another group.'

'What do you mean?' the other human said. 'And how do you know it's female?'

'When female spider monkeys come into maturity, they leave their natal groups and seek out new ones. The males stay, so unless they have a background like Kido here, who was originally taken from the wild by the pet trade, it's rare for males to be on their own. Kido only remains with us because the rest of his natal group were all captured. Unfortunately, the traders who were shipping them crashed the van they were using and both they and the monkeys all died from the impact. Kido was the only one to escape, and when we found him he had a deep gash on his leg. After we treated him, we released him in the hopes that he would find somewhere to go, but he tends to stay close by.'

'So what will you do with the female?' the other human asked, pointing at Hyda. Hyda looked at it and it threw her more fruit. She grabbed it hungrily.

The female human smiled. 'As long as she's healthy, which she appears to be, then we will leave her be. *Unless* she decides to stay around here with Kido, which I have a feeling has crossed his mind.' It turned its gaze to him as he offered his fruit to Hyda.

Hyda took it from Kido gladly. 'Perhaps you're right,' she said. 'These humans appear safe, and the food is good.'

'Will you stay, then?' Kido asked hopefully.

Hyda shook her head. 'I will carry on searching for a new family group. But,' she said, noticing his eyes grow dull, 'if I can't find one, or I dislike the one I find, then I may return here. If it is necessary, we may start our own family group.'

Kido looked at her, beaming.

'*If* it is necessary,' she said, sternly.

Kido's head drooped, but he gave her some more fruit. She took it.

Second Body

I MOVE my gaze from the ceiling to look over at the door, where the slight shadow of Dr Zaki lingers, waiting for me to reply to his knock.

'I suppose you want my blood again?' I ask, turning my head left so the sensors on my bed register the movement. The top end rises up so that I'm in a sitting position.

Zaki takes this as a welcome and comes into my sparse room, a smile on his face. 'You make me sound like some kind of vampire,' he says, checking my drip and preparing a syringe to take my blood.

I sniff. 'A vampire would have put me out of my misery long before now.'

He raises an eyebrow. 'You've got the same self-pity in your voice that my daughter has,' he replies, inserting the needle.

'What reason has she got pity herself? I bet *she* isn't paralysed from the neck down.'

'No, but she's a teenager too. All teenagers have problems. True, you've been through far more difficulties than most, but that doesn't mean you can't be positive. You've still got your wits, after all.'

I open my mouth to protest, but he holds up his hand. 'What would you say if I said you might be able to walk again; to sculpt, even?'

'I'd say you were a lying bastard who's toying with my hopes. I know there's no way any kind of surgery can help me,' I spit back, noticing with annoyance that my colostomy bag is full. Zaki sees it too, and rings for a nurse to come and empty it.

'I'm not talking about having surgery,' he continues, once the nurse has finished, fleeing from the room as though I might shout profanities again, like the time she made a complete mess of my bed sheets.

'There's a new kind of technology that I believe will help you. We call it Second Body, and if you agree to try it, you will be the first person to do so in the world.'

It's my turn to raise an eyebrow. 'So, what does it do, then?'

'Before I answer that, may I ask if you've ever played any virtual-reality games that have come out in the last five years?'

'Don't be stupid. My parents never let me play

any kind of games, especially after I became known as some silly child prodigy.'

'But do you know how they work?' he presses.

'I know they involve putting on some kind of helmet. One of my friends used to play them. She said that when you were inside the game, you had your own virtual body that responded just like your real one. You can even smell and taste things.' I look at him and notice he's grinning. 'What does this have to do with anything, anyway?'

'Well, Second Body technology is based heavily off of those games. However, instead of allowing you to move around in a virtual world, Second Body lets you move around in this one. The idea is that you put on a helmet and then your consciousness is transferred into an artificial body.'

'Like a robot?'

'Yes. But it wouldn't look like one. It would be very similar to how you look now so, in theory, you could go anywhere you wanted with it and no one would know. Of course, your real body would have to stay here in the hospital so we can monitor you, and make sure your health doesn't suffer, but—'

'I'll do it. It's a weird concept, but if I can get out of this loathsome bed for even a day, then it'll be worth it. What do I have to do?'

Zaki looks awkward. 'I do need your parents' approval before we can actually go forward with any of the major preparations …'

I laugh, somewhere between amusement and

rage. 'If you think they'll bother coming to see you, then you're an idiot. You know they abandoned me here as soon as they found out I'd never be able to sculpt again.'

'It's true, they aren't the most forthcoming people I know. But if you really want this, then I promise I'll convince them for you.' He looks sincere, but I say nothing. If he really believes that, then he *is* an idiot. 'Just trust me, okay? Now, as to what we can do in the mean time, I'll have the designer of your Second Body come in and speak with you. We can start your training, too.'

'Training? What kind of training?'

He doesn't reply, but irritatingly taps his finger to the side of his nose.

———

I hardly see Zaki over the next few days, despite asking everyone who comes in what's going on. Finally, after the seventh time that I've spat out my food when nobody answers, he arrives with what looks like a strange biker helmet.

'This is for your training,' he says, holding it up so I can get a closer look. 'It's synced up to an online virtual-reality game. It's the latest one out and uses the closest technology publicly available to the Second Body tech. Hopefully by playing it, you'll get used to using this headgear and using your mind to control a body other than your real one.'

'So my training consists of playing games?' I say. 'That doesn't sound very professional.'

'I suppose it's unusual, but this is the only way to get you used to the technology that we'll be using. Play it. Have fun.'

I roll my eyes. Playing a game sounds like a waste of time, but then all I've been able to do since the accident *is* to waste time. If it helps me with the Second Body tech, then maybe I shouldn't complain.

I allow Zaki to fit the headgear over my hair and face. It feels surprisingly warm. I can also hear a slight buzzing, presumably from all the gadgetry inside it.

'Just relax,' he begins, but then I can no longer hear him, or see the ceiling of my room. Even the smell of disinfectant that usually clogs my nostrils has been replaced with the scent of damp pine needles.

I open my eyes, without knowing I'd closed them, and see that I'm in a large forest clearing, with a single glass mirror floating upright just above the ground in front of me. I can tell what I'm seeing isn't real, because everything has a definite stylistic touch to it, and when I peer into the mirror, the face gazing back at me belongs to some kind of elf.

There are buttons on the mirror for adjusting not only my body, but also the game settings. I look down at my hands. It's been so long since I've been able to move them … does my brain even still have the connections to do it?

Slowly, I think about wriggling my fingers, but the virtual body was obviously designed to feel much lighter than my real one, and I end up hitting myself hard in the thigh. I find tears on my cheeks, unsure if they are from mirth or joy.

I can move again, even if it is in a game.

———

After a month of 'training', Zaki introduces me to the chief designer in charge of the team that will be making my Second Body, a woman in her thirties called Elis. She has purple hair and a Celtic knot tattooed on her wrist, just like the ones I used to carve onto my sculptures and pottery.

The scent of clay and slip comes to me as I stare at it; all the hours I've spent shaping and moulding coming sharply back. I can even feel the wetness of the clay on my fingertips.

Elis coughs uncomfortably. 'Dr Zaki tells me that you're quite the sculpting prodigy.'

I snort. 'I was, before this.' I nod at my pathetic body.

'You'd like to sculpt again?'

'Of course I would,' I snap.

'Then I'll help you. For the Second Body to work for you, I need to know everything. Your passion for sculpting means that the arms and hands of

When The Bard Came Visiting

your Second Body need to be the same weight as your real ones, if you want to be able to use your skills straight away.'

She continues, telling me that once my parents give their permission, she will come back and take photos and plaster casts of my arms.

I've completely forgotten about needing their permission. Zaki hasn't said a word about them, so I'd presumed he hadn't gotten anywhere. But now that I've spoken with Elis, I know that this really is what I want. Getting them to sign the paperwork is vital.

Three months pass without any news, but then Zaki appears again grinning like some idiot school kid. He doesn't say anything, but simply holds out his computer tablet. I can just make out the permission documents; signed digitally with both of my parents' signatures.

'How did you …?'

'I mentioned that the Second Body project would let you sculpt again. Couldn't sign it quick enough.'

'Huh,' I sniff. 'If I can sculpt again, then they can sell my work for extortionate prices, just like they used to. I should have known they'd sign it for that.'

Zaki shrugs. 'No-one has perfect parents. Besides, until we get past the prototype stages, I don't think making sculptures for sale is an option. Maybe you can keep them as a keepsake of your rehabilitation.'

For once, I smile.

———

The next year is busy. Zaki and Elis come in regularly to take measurements and update me on their progress. In total, it takes about thirteen months from getting permission to the first prototype run.

It's today.

They wheel me into a room similar to a morgue, except that there is only one body laid out, covered in a sheet. It takes me a moment to realise that this is it. My Second Body.

As I get closer, Zaki raises my head so I can see properly as he pulls back the sheet. If I wasn't half expecting it, I would faint. My Second Body is almost identical to me, even having the same scar on my nose from where I had chicken pox as a kid.

'What do you think?' Elis asks, coming into the room holding the same type of headgear I've been using to play the game, except sleeker.

'I feel like I've been cloned,' I say, still staring at it.

She laughs. 'I suppose you would. So, are you ready?'

I look at her, then at Zaki, who nods, and finally back to my Second Body, the corners of my mouth twitching up. 'I might give it a go.'

Zaki lowers my head again so that I'm lying flat,

and Elis fits the headgear onto me. 'It's no different to when you play the game. Just relax and let the headgear do the work.'

I grunt and rest my head against the pillow, but then she's leaning over me, asking if I'm alright.

'Of course I'm alright,' I say. 'Nothing's happened yet.'

Then I realise I've just sat up. She and Zaki gape at me.

I look down at my stomach, feeling cold. I'm only in my underwear, and my colostomy bag is gone. Hardly daring to, I turn my head to the side and see myself lying down on a bed opposite, with the headgear still covering my face.

'No. No way,' I say. 'This can't be real. It … it *feels* just like my real body. I don't …'

Zaki manages to close his mouth and hands me some clothes. 'We never expected you to have such control so quickly. A twitch of the fingers, maybe, or a nod …' He coughs. 'There's a, er, ceramics studio in our rehabilitation centre, if you—'

Before he can finish speaking, I jump off the table and rush from the room, pulling the clothes on as I go.

Turn Around the Other Way

THE SOUND of footsteps rouses me from my sleep, heeled shoes running along the hall. My clock reads three in the morning. It must have been quite some party.

It's unusual for her to go straight to Rich's room, though. Usually she needs to vomit or sober herself up first. I can't complain, my room is right next to the bathroom, and if she's missing out on that particular ritual tonight, that's fine with me.

I hear his bedroom door open with a bang. There's a startled cry, followed by raised voices. I can't help it, I have to go and look.

I slip the covers off my legs and slide out of bed, making no noise as I tread on the soft carpet. My door creaks as I open it, but I doubt they can hear anything above the racket they're making.

I carry on along the hall, reaching the door to

the master bedroom and resting my ear against it. The tapestry on the wall flutters. I start, but realise it's just a breeze. I turn my attention back to the door.

'Don't give me that rubbish, Richard, I know you've been sleeping with her!' Michelle slurs. I bend to look through the keyhole and see her standing just in front of his bed. Her make-up is smudged and her short green dress has a dark stain on it, probably red wine.

'Sleeping with her? Don't be ridiculous, she's my brother's widow!' he says from somewhere be-yond my limited view. By the mini bar, I'd guess.

'That never stopped you before. I know you had a thing for one of your cousins.'

'Michelle, please, we were children, and she was a very *distant* cousin anyway. Believe me, there's no other woman in my life more important to me than you. Haven't I proved that several times over?'

'Oh yes, you buy me jewellery and clothes, and ship me off on expensive spa weekends, but that's not love, is it?'

'What more do you want? You know I work all week, and on weekends I see you as much as I can.'

There's silence while Michelle ponders his words. I can almost see the thoughts trying to swim through her befuddled mind and come to a sensible conclusion, but then she screws up her face and lets out a nausea-inducing wail. Again, the tapestry next to me quivers. I examine it, wondering if her astounding vocal talents are causing some kind of tremor effect, then the tapestry is still.

'Liar! You don't need to work at all, you own two companies! They bring in all your money,' Michelle says, at last stopping her awful noise.

Now I know it's wrong to judge someone's intelligence on a single sentence, especially when they're so plastered; it's a wonder they can even talk at all, but good god woman, have you no concept of how businesses are managed?

'Companies need to be maintained, my dear. I can't just hire someone else to oversee how they're run; that's how things go wrong. Indeed, that's how I managed to buy them out in the first place.'

'Well, you could at least cut down your hours, instead of spending all your spare time with her.'

Mentioning me, again? Where had she gotten *that* idea? As Rich said, I'm his brother's widow. Now that Jon's gone, I have no other family apart from my brother Markus, who's employed as Rich's butler anyway, and since I was already familiar with the house and grounds, Rich asked if I'd like to live here. It's true I like him, but not in any sort of romantic way. I see him as another brother, nothing more.

'Listen to me, Michelle. What makes you think I'm having an affair—with Jody, too?'

'I've seen the way you look at her. The secret smiles, the twinkle in your eyes. Oh yes, I've noticed. One of your shirts also smells of that sickly-sweet perfume she wears.'

'I can explain that. The shirt had a hole in it, and you were busy, so I asked her if she could mend it for me. As for those so-called secret smiles, you know perfectly well that Jody and I are good friends and we share lots of jokes about how similar I am to Jon.'

I can hear the sorrow in his voice as he mentions his brother. Jon's death was so sudden, it cut both our hearts to pieces. It's scarcely a year since his funeral, and Rich is the only one who I can share my pain with. How does Michelle expect us to act, when we both need to be consoled by the other?

'You really want me to believe that this is all because of Jon? Get over it, Rich, he's dead. I'm *not*, so pay attention to me!'

Something made of glass shatters on the floor; I see shards of it skitter towards Michelle's feet. Her jaw is hanging slack in shock. Rich must have smashed a bottle. How he stopped himself from throwing it at her after that remark, I'm not sure. *I* certainly wouldn't have held back. In fact, if it wasn't for the fact that I know barging in would only make things worse, I'd have punched her already.

'Get out.'

With those two words, Rich projects enough authority to make even Michelle obey. She scuttles towards the door quicker than I can move out the way but, as it opens, a pair of slender arms grab me and pull me behind the tapestry. Michelle stampedes past without any idea I was ever there.

I turn in the darkness, sensing that I'm in some kind of narrow corridor. Someone's standing close to me. I catch a whiff of spiced aftershave. 'Markus?'

'Who else would it be, little sis?' he replies, lighting a candle so that I can see his clean-shaven face. He nods to the surrounding area. 'Being a butler *does* have its privileges. You get to know about all the secret passages in an old manor house like this.'

'What are you doing up this late? Or early, I should say,' I ask, remembering the time.

'Same as you. I was curious about what was going on with those two. I never expected her to go that far, though,' he says. 'Breakfast tomorrow should prove to be interesting.'

———

Breakfast is indeed proving to be interesting. We're all seated together in the dining room while Markus, dutiful as ever, and with no indication that he has any idea of what went on last night, serves our food.

Michelle looks ill, but that isn't enough to stop her giving me filthy looks. Rich, in his seat at the head of the table, catches her in the act and dryly announces how fine the weather is today. I cast my gaze out the window; it's grey and stormy.

Abruptly, Michelle stands up and takes out a cigarette from the silver case she always keeps on her person. She lights it, and taking a deep drag, walks around the table to stand beside me and exhales the lot in my face. I cough and waft it away with the newspaper.

'Is there something you want to say to me?' I ask, also standing. I hold my hand up to silence Rich as he starts to say something. I know I shouldn't react to her childish behaviour, but frankly, after what she said last night, I'm ready to have my say.

'You could put it that way, yes. I *know* what you've been up to with my husband.'

'Really? Then perhaps you should tell me so that I might know, too.'

She sneers. 'He's having an affair with you.'

I snort. 'An affair? How original. When did this supposed affair take place?'

'Don't play innocent with me, Jody. Your perfume is all over his clothes, and ever since you got here he's been distant from me.'

'Michelle, when I came here Jon had just died. Rich was in pain just like me. Of course he's been distant. As for his shirt, it's like he told you last night, I repaired it for him.'

Okay, that last part wasn't wise.

'You were listening? How dare you eavesdrop on us! I bet you had your ear to the door, fishing for every word we said. You must have been hoping we'd split so you could move in like the snake you are and have him all to yourself!'

'Michelle,' I say in a pained voice, 'for the last time, there is nothing going on between myself and Rich. Believe me.'

'Believe you? Why should I? You think I'm an idiot, nothing more than white trash. You're so bad at hiding it that I wouldn't be surprised if everyone knows how you feel about me.'

'Alright, it's true that you're not the type of person I can take to easily, but I've never thought of you as trash.' Though I *do* think she's and idiot. 'I try my best to get on with you, but you certainly make it difficult when you go around accusing me of everything. Last week it was spilling paint on your new carpet, now it's this.'

'Jody, you are one patronising b—'

'Michelle, will you keep your mouth shut and listen for a change? Jody-and-I-are-not-having-an-affair!' Rich interjects, speaking through clenched teeth.

'You're wasting your breath, Rich,' I say.

'You're both lying,' Michelle hisses, proving my point.

'Why would we lie to you?' I ask.

'Why? *Why?* Because you think I'm just some silly tart and Richard just thinks I want his money,

so stop insisting that there's nothing going on between you two and own up. I've seen you walking
around the grounds together, arm in arm—'

'They're not lying, Michelle. You're just so para-
noid that you're seeing things that aren't there.'

She whips round to see Markus standing by the
door with a tray of tea. His knuckles are white, he's
gripping the tray hard. I frown. He's angry. Markus
never gets angry.

'What would you know?' Michelle spits at him.

'Jody would never do such a thing. She's still in
love with Jon; she always will be. However, seeing as
you're so hell bent on wanting to accuse someone,
perhaps you should accuse me.'

I notice the colour drain from Rich's face.
What's going on here?

'Markus, perhaps you should just serve the tea
and let me handle this,' Rich says quietly.

'Oh, no,' Michelle says. 'I want to know *exactly*
what he means by that.'

'I mean what I said. Maybe you should accuse
me of having an affair with Rich. Because it's true.
He's just too shy to admit it,' Markus says bluntly.

Well, that's a surprise. Not to mention I feel like
a lousy sister. Markus knows so much about me, and
I thought I knew everything about him. Yet I had
no idea he was gay. How could something as important as this have slipped by me?

I do know this, though: Markus has always had
great timing. The horror on Michelle's face at this

sudden revelation will stick with us for years, and I think even Rich was glad when she left the manor barely ten minutes later with her suitcase fully packed.

Honestly, how he ever ended up with her in the first place I'll never know. At least now he and Markus can actually be happy. And, for the first time since Jon died, I think I can be, too.

Miko's Courage

MIKO SNIFFED at the night air, then began scraping at the ground in search of tasty morsels. As a pacarana, one of the largest rodents in the world, he should have been well accustomed to foraging, even if it meant climbing trees. Alas, for Miko, climbing was one thing he could never do, for the fear that gripped him whenever he tried was too great to overcome his hunger.

When he'd been a pup, all the other pacaranas his age had scurried up the mighty trunks as though there was nothing easier, but when Miko tried, his head swam and he lost his grip. And so he fell. Again. And again. And again.

The other pups found it hilarious, but there was nothing he could do about it. Ashamed of himself, he'd tried to run away, but his mother had brought him back and lectured him for days.

'Not everyone can climb trees the first time. Sometimes, you just have to work at it,' she'd said. It was alright for *her* to say—she'd set the record for climbing by scurrying up one of the tallest trees around when she was only a few weeks old.

For years, Miko tried in secret to get over his phobia, but no sooner had he got his hind feet off the ground than the dizziness swept over him and he fell back to the ground. Now he quivered if he even went near a tree.

However, finding food on the forest floor was growing increasingly difficult. There just wasn't enough. Some days didn't find anything. They were especially hard, as his stomach refused to stop rumbling.

There wasn't even anyone Miko could turn to for help, for they had all mysteriously disappeared. The only other pacarana he ever saw was an aggressive old git called Ka, and when Miko came across him, he quickly turned back the other way.

Confronting Ka was not a wise idea, particularly if the bully was hungry. He would often attack without reason, as Miko had found out some weeks earlier.

As it happened, Miko could smell Ka just a little way in front of him. He stayed well back, rummaging around a pile of wide, thick leaves to see if any were edible, pretending that he hadn't noticed him there.

Ka chattered his teeth. It was no good; he'd already caught Miko's scent. In a few moments he would be upon him, and there was nowhere for Miko to run.

But Ka didn't come. Miko waited, frozen to the spot, but after a few minutes, curiosity got the better of him. He crept forwards so that he was in Ka's line of sight.

Yet instead of Ka, Miko saw a tall creature with pale skin and no fur, standing on two legs. *A human.* In its hand, writhing and trying to bite, was Ka. But the human had extra skin on its hands that made Ka's efforts fruitless.

Miko didn't know what to do. He didn't like Ka for sure, but that didn't mean he deserved to be caught. What did the human want? Where would it take him?

On the spur of the moment, Miko made his choice. He ran around the back of the human and sank his teeth into its tendon—hard. The human lurched forward, barking out a harsh cry, and dropped Ka on the ground.

'Ka, run!' Miko shouted, pushing the stunned pacarana as far away from the human as they could get.

Then other humans appeared, and at the calls of the one Miko had bitten, they chased the two pacaranas. Running under limbs and snatching hands, Miko and Ka strove on until both of them were on the verge of collapse.

Their pace slowed, but the humans were almost upon them. 'We must climb,' Ka said, the rush of adrenaline causing him to regain his senses. He scurried off to the left and up a tall tree, so bearded with leaves that it was impossible to see him.

'I can't,' shouted Miko desperately. 'I've never been able to climb.'

'All pacaranas can climb,' Ka snapped back. 'Don't think about it, just do it!'

The humans were close now; if Miko didn't move soon, he wouldn't stand a chance. He ran, turning left as Ka had done and, with fear of capture overpowering that of his phobia, he launched himself up the tree like a ball of reverse lightning.

He watched as the humans charged past, completely unaware of what had just happened. Breathing a sigh of relief, Miko promptly lost his balance and slid from his branch, but Ka grabbed his paw with his mouth and dragged him back up.

'Sit still,' he said, with an agitated chatter of teeth. Miko obeyed, not only because he was nervous of what Ka might do to him, but because he was too worn out to do anything else.

They sat in silence for hours, slowly getting their energy back. Luckily, the tree they were in was covered in rain droplets, which they drank readily.

'Why did you save me, boy?' Ka asked after a while.

Miko looked at him, trying to lift the fog of being up so high from his brain. 'I'm not sure, exactly,' he said slowly. 'I didn't know what they were going to do with you, and it scared me.'

'You didn't know?' Ka said, taken aback. He thought for a moment. 'Perhaps it's better that way … not knowing.'

'You mean you *do* know what they were going to do?' Miko asked.

Ka nodded. 'They were going to eat me.'

Miko nearly fell off the tree again. 'E-eat you? But why?' he asked, astounded.

'Because they are creatures that eat other creatures. We eat leaves, stems and fruits to survive. Yet they eat flesh, skin and bone. They do not care that there are so little of us left; they will hunt us until we are no more,' Ka said, both despair and anger in his voice. 'My mate and pups were taken by them months ago. I never saw them again.'

'I'm sorry,' Miko said sincerely. 'Are humans really the reason there are hardly any of us left? Did they take my mother and my brothers and sisters?'

'I do not know for sure, but it is likely,' Ka replied.

Miko began to whimper. The thought of his family dead made his heart crumple.

'It's no using crying, boy,' Ka said harshly. 'It won't bring anyone back. All we can do is run from the humans so they don't catch us, too.'

Miko sniffed and shook his head. 'No, there must be something we can do—'

'Like what?'Ka scoffed. 'We're small and weak

and few in number. They're large and strong, and there are many of them. I have seen more humans of late than I have of any other creature that hunts us. There is no way we can stop them.'

'You're right,' Miko said. 'We might not be able to stop them completely, but we can try. They may think they know this forest, but surely they're too enormous to see the things we see. We can surprise them, like I surprised the one that captured you.'

'Don't be ridiculous. I'm thankful for what you did, boy, but you should have thought about your own safety. If they'd caught up with us, then we would both have been captured and taken away to be eaten. Trying to save more of our kind by running headfirst into danger like that is nothing but suicide. You were lucky this time, but if you try it again, your luck might fail.'

Ka spoke so fiercely that Miko swallowed. Still, he gritted his teeth, forming his resolve. 'Maybe I will lose my luck and get caught, but I have to try.'

'If that's your decision, then so be it. I don't want any part in it,' Ka said, finality in his tone.

Miko sighed, knowing it was useless to try and persuade him, and hurried down the tree again. It made him woozy still, but now that he knew he could do it, the fear didn't grip him as hard.

He sniffed the ground. The humans had been gone for several hours now, but even so, their scent was still fresh. Miko decided to follow it.

Sure, it would be dangerous, but if the humans

were out to hunt other pacaranas, then they would lead him directly to his brethren. He hoped it wasn't too late.

The forest floor was dense with leaves and roots, and Miko could feel the eyes of many other creatures following him. There was a crackle above the treetops, higher up than Miko could see, and a flash of bright light illuminated everything around him.

Rain came down, not in a soft mist, but in great heavy splashes. He had to hurry. If he didn't, then the scent of the humans would get washed away along with his hope of catching up to them.

He sped up, despite being so hungry that he thought he might faint, twisting and turning as the scent trail did. Despite the rain, it appeared to be getting stronger. He must be close.

Suddenly, the forest opened out into a small clearing where the scent accosted him so sharply, it sent him reeling.

There were pouches made from animal skins (thankfully Miko didn't recognise any of them), filled with dried fruit and nuts and strips of meat. It made Miko sick to look at them, so he turned his head to a pile of bamboo crates stacked in one corner. Most were empty or filled with creatures that were already beyond saving, but at the very top, cowering into balls, were three pacarana pups.

Miko hesitated. He looked around to make sure that there were no humans hidden behind the bushes or anywhere else, then took a deep breath and scampered up the stack of crates to the top.

The pups mewled at him, petrified. 'It's alright,' he cooed. 'I'm going to get you out of here.'

He assessed the crate, trying to find a way to open it, yet there wasn't one. Instead, he bared his teeth and chomped on the bamboo, hard. It took several minutes, but eventually he managed to bite through it.

He made the opening wider by scrapping at it with his paws, gently lifted the pups out one by one.

Slowly, they made their way down the stack of crates, wet from the rain. Miko watched the pups carefully, making sure that they didn't slip, and occasionally giving them a nudge to stop them losing their balance. They reached the ground, safe and uninjured, but just as Miko was about to lead them away, a large shadow fell over him.

In one quick swoop, the human grabbed him by his hind legs and held him upside down. Miko squirmed, screaming and whining so loudly that the pups scarpered away into the bushes. The human took out giant, shiny claw that glinted in the first light of dawn.

Miko closed his eyes.

Then he found he was falling, and with a crash, landed on the ground. The human was snatched at his rump and tried to stomp the ground with its feet at the same time.

Miko blinked. Scurrying by was Ka, nipping at

its flesh with every chance he got. He glanced over at Miko and met his eyes. They could do this.

Miko evaded the human's grasp and dashed over to aide Ka. Faster and faster they ran, the human spinning around with them. Then, from giddiness and the pain of Ka's bites, it feel to the ground.

Seeing their chance, Miko and Ka ran off into the bushes where the pups had gone. They were still there, cowering under the leaves. The two adults wasted no time picking them up by the scruffs of their necks and running with them deep into the forest, putting as much distance between themselves and the humans as possible.

Eventually, they stopped to catch their breath.

'I thought you said you didn't want any part in rescuing others?' Miko said to Ka.

Ka look away. 'I knew you would get your idiot self caught. Besides, I owed you,' he said. He sniffed in disgust as he looked at the pups. 'Now look what trouble you've got me into. What are we supposed to do with them?'

'Well, I doubt they have any family left,' Miko said, as an idea caught in his mind. He glanced at Ka, his eyes sparkling mischievously. 'I guess it's up to us to raise them.'

Ka stared at Miko as the pups leaned against his fur. 'I'm too old for this,' he muttered.

Expectations of the Homosapien

September 12ᵗʰ, 1896

Dearest Nephew,

Please stop pestering your dear mother about my work, for she does tire of it so. I have searched through my old journals and thus found the entries you will find enclosed. Hopefully, they shall answer any questions you may have. If that is not the case, however, send me a telegram and I shall respond in good time.

Give your mother my best,
Marcellus

April 16ᵗʰ, 1882

I have taught as Fellow of the College for five years

this day and, though I am deeply content, having intelligent students and commendably sized quarters, I cannot help but feel as though something is missing from my life. I admit, I am now reaching the age when one usually settles down to marriage, but I fear it is something other than that.

April 22nd, 1882

Whilst breakfasting this morning, I did read in the newspaper that the esteemed naturalist, Charles Darwin, died this past week at his house in Kent. His passing has saddened me, for he has been influential on my view of life and all things natural. However, death must come to us all and should I, like he, reach the age of three and seventy, I shall be most content.

April 23rd, 1882

Upon making notes for my lecture tomorrow which, as my students may comment, are sorely needed due to my tendencies to stray terribly far from the subject, I happened to gaze out of the window of my chambers. There, to my delight, I spotted a mouse scurrying along the flagstones of the courtyard. I did worry for a moment, for the College has a cat in residence, but such was the colour of the rodent's fur and its minute size that, upon reaching the hedge, it all but disappeared from view. I never cease to be fascinated by nature.

April 26th, 1882

I have just returned from the Master's office, for he did call me there after dinner this evening. It is rare to be summoned such, and so I went with no small degree of nervousness. I shall recount our meeting as best I can:

'Master,' said I, stepping inside. 'You wish to discuss something with me?'

'Indeed, Marcellus,' said he. 'Please, be seated and help yourself to the decanter.'

I sat.

'Now, then,' continued he. 'Jones informed me yesterday that you have been straying from your subject. Is this correct?'

'Yes, sir,' said I, my body rigid under his strong gaze. 'I spoke about the work of Charles Darwin, to further explain an answer that I did give to one of my students.'

He surveyed me for a few moments, and I had felt quite the schoolboy again. 'Tell me, *Marcellus, is evolution something you wish to teach?*'

'Yes, Master, I find it fascinating! Still, I fail to see how it would be possible; after all, I am merely a professor of geology, I have no formal education in the matter.'

'You speak true, of course,' said he, nodding. 'Yet I wonder if lecturing here is all that you are destined for.'

I drew an involuntary intake of breath, and exhaled my words so quickly that I had to repeat them.

'Surely, sir, you do not mean to have me laid off?'

The Master chortled. 'Marcellus, had I wished to have you laid off, I would not have invited you here so politely. Be reassured, sir, that your position is safe. Though you may soon find yourself travelling.'

'Travelling, Master? For what reason?' asked I.

'To teach, sir. Despite your lack of formal education on the science of evolution, you may still teach it. Teach the commoners; ordinary men and women who find themselves ignorant of such things simply because their pockets are empty.'

'The working classes?' said I, unsure of whether I had heard him correctly.

'Yes, Marcellus. Knowledge and education should be for all, as I am sure you will agree. I shall let you think on the matter for a few days,' said he.

And so I took my leave and returned here to ponder on it. Oh, for the suddenness of it all!

April 27th, 1882

I feel that I must accept the Master's proposal, for

who can know when such an opportunity will arise again? Though I would have preferred to teach evolution within the College, I know it would truly be impossible without any formal training. However, as the Master did say, education should be for all. I am sure that teaching those of the working classes will be a valuable experience, for it seems like an age since I have been in the company of non-academics. I feel the change shall be refreshing!

May 3*rd*, 1882 - Morning

The carriage arrived promptly at 6.30am, and by 6.36am had departed with myself and my luggage safely onboard. It jolted less than I had expected, having not been in one for some time and, in fact, I felt it to be a rather relaxing motion.

At 6.46am, the carriage pulled up outside the station and, with my luggage in tow, I entered the bustling, glass-roofed building and made my way to the 7.05am train bound for King's Lynn. The station was crowded, not only with people, but with black smoke and steam. Despite the jostling and confusion, I managed to find the correct train within a few moments. As it would only be a short journey, and due to the College's increasingly limited funds, I found that my ticket was for second class, and so made my way to the compartments there. Prior to today, I had not been on a train in some years, so my expectations of how the compartment should be furnished were somewhat low, but I was pleasantly surprised to see that the seats were cushioned, if not a little hard. However, now that the train is underway, I have noticed a distinct lack of legroom, and if I was a taller man, I feel this journey would prove rather uncomfortable.

May 3rd, 1882 - Late Morning

At 8.44am the train reached King's Lynn station, and as I disembarked I found it to be almost an exact double of the station in Cambridge. I supposed that the design must serve the railway so well that all stations would use it thus.

After checking with the warden for directions to the boarding house I would be staying at, I made my way there, passing through the morning market. My willpower was sorely tested as I passed the stall selling freshly baked loaves, for their aromatic smell tempted me most dearly. Still, I held fast and carried on.

I took the first left, and found the boarding house much as the warden had said. It seemed, on appearance, to not even be large enough for one boarder, but my preconceptions proved, rather thankfully, to be false. Inside, the hall was large, and many doors went off to the sides. No sooner had I glanced about, however, than a woman of middle years came out to meet me.

'You are the Professor, are you not?' said she, in a tone most crisp and efficient. I answered that indeed I was, and she told me that she was Miss Kathleen Jenkins, sole owner of the boarding house.

'Follow me, Professor, and I shall show you to your lodgings,' said she, and made to pick up my suitcase.' I informed her that it was not necessary.

'As you wish,' replied she, most curtly.

She led me past all the doors I had taken note of, and turned through an archway of sorts that was all but invisible from the entrance. There was a short staircase just a few steps past, and my room was through the single door at the top. 'I keep this room for scholars such as yourself. I find that you are people who…prefer your own company. You should have everything you need.' She paused briefly. 'You are to be staying for the week?'

'Quite so, I plan to travel around the whole of Eng—'

'Then we shall settle the bill on the day of your departure, if it pleases you,' said she, in that same crisp manner as before. 'Breakfast is at seven, supper at six. If you require luncheon, I must be notified at least three hours prior, and the cost shall be added to your total. I prefer not to serve latecomers, Professor.'

Her manner was most matronly, but I had not taken

great offence, for truly anyone who wishes their business to succeed must stand by stout rules.

The room I have rented is of modest size, though smaller than my beloved study at the College. Over to the far wall sits the bed, the mattress decently clean and of suitable firmness, and a small table on which I have placed my copy of On the Origin of Species (where, should I wish, I may reach for it before turning in). The desk at which I now sit is situated by the window, whereby plenty of light penetrates the room so that I may write without candle or lamp.

Ah, but now hunger calls, and I must explore the town for a fine place to lunch.

May 4th, 1882 - Morning

Today I shall give my first lecture in King's Lynn, and though I am but a stranger here, it seems that word has spread as to the subject I will be teaching. Yesterday, while exploring the town, I had a doctor approach me and shake my hand and, with his tongue tripping over his words, tell me how exciting it was to have a professor such as myself willing to address all peoples on such an important subject. We spoke briefly on it and parted with a smile, but not two moments later did the fine woman from the nearby hat shop turn her attention away from her customers to strike me across the cheek, before calling me a blasphemer.

I am aware that many who have heard of Darwin's theories do not as yet understand them, but to go thus far to insult a pure stranger? It is enough to make my nerves for tonight most unsettled. Still, I have all the day to prepare, so I shall take care to word my lecture most carefully.

May 4th, 1882 - Evening

I have just returned from giving my lecture at the town hall. Perhaps half the room was full, which was rather more than I had expected, given the treatment I received yesterday. I was also rather surprised to see Miss Jenkins attending, and standing next to her was none other than the woman from the hat shop. I admit that upon seeing them both there, my throat did tighten a little, something that has not troubled me since my first days lecturing at the College. I also noticed the good doctor there, and the warden from the railway station. All waited patiently as I gathered my notes together and took my place before them.

'Ladies and gentlemen,' I had begun. 'First of all, good evening to you. I thank you for attending this evening, for I understand that your schedules may be somewhat heavy. I am Professor Marcellus Kingston, Fellow of Clare College at Cambridge

University, and I humbly come before you tonight to speak on a matter which has been most influential to my thinking and my work: evolution.'

I had paused then, to take a glance around the room, and I was pleased to see their attention held fully.

'Now, let me take but a moment,' said I. 'I am sure many of you have heard of evolution, but what does it truly mean? And what is this talk of natural selection, you might ask? Ladies and gentlemen, tonight I shall answer these questions.

'Let us begin with an examination of, let us say, the budgerigar. The wild budgerigar is a bird native to the country of Australia and is, on average, a mere four inches in length. The plumage is green, and they have a light frame, which allows them to move with speed. Now, let me give the specifications of its domestic counterpart. The domestic budgerigar can grow up to six inches in length, the frame is heavier, and the plumage can vary in colour greatly, not just in differing shades of green, but also with yellow and blue varieties, with many more variations being found as we speak.

'But what is it that causes these variations, ladies and gentlemen? This variation under domestication? It is the careful selection of breeding pairs by the breeder. They set their trained eyes out for slight differences between individual birds, perhaps a differentiation of pattern, or a broadening of the forehead, or any other quality pleasing to the eye, and pair that bird with another of similar qualities. Thus, offspring with those qualities are born and able to be bred from, producing another variation of the breed.

'We see this with many other animals as well. Take the dog, for example. If we want to procure a bloodline of dogs that are strong, loyal and calm natured, do we not look for those qualities in individuals, and then, once found, breed from them?'

Though I was sure that many in the room had no first-hand experience of breeding domestic birds or dogs, I was glad to see a small nod of approval from the crowd, most notably from the warden from the railway and, surprisingly, Miss Jenkins. Encouraged, I began to explain further on the delicate process of breeding for particular traits, and then to how this related to natural selection.

'Ladies and gentlemen, now that we know how these variations occur within domestic creatures, how then do variations occur with their wild counterparts, and perhaps more pertinently, for what reason? Surely there are no competitions between flocks of budgerigars with a prize for most flamboyant plumage?'

A few members of the crowd chortled at this, and the muscles in my neck did ease slightly.

'Indeed, variation within nature is not managed wilfully by the species concerned. No, variation within nature occurs due to the very circumstances within which the species lives. If a species of animal or plant native to a warm climate is then moved to a cooler one, the species will either acclimatise to this cooler climate, or die out. Another example is diet: if there were a lack of prey for our dear friend the fox, then it too would either have to adapt or die out. Of course, I do not mean to say that such adaptation occurs immediately; it takes many years and generations of offspring for a species to change. It is this, my dear people, that forms the basic principle of evolution. Change to a species over many years due to environmental fluctuations.'

I had then taken but a momentary pause, but before I could continue, the woman from the hat shop, who was sitting next to Miss Jenkins, called out to me. 'Sir, this theory of yours is … interesting, but may I put to you the words of the Bible? Does it not say in Genesis 1:24 that the Holy Father created all animals as they are now? I do not seem to remember any mention of them changing over time,' said she, and I did notice a glint in her eye as she spoke.

'Thank you for your contribution, Madam, but I am afraid that you are mistaken. The Bible states, and I quote, "And God said, Let the earth bring forth the living creature after his kind, cattle, and creeping thing, and beast of the earth after his kind: and it was so." There is nothing pertaining to animals created as we know them now.'

'I did not expect you to know the Bible so thoroughly, Professor,' replied she, after a small intake of breath. 'I admit I am impressed, but I must still make my point. This evolution, as you call it, makes no appearance in the Bible, and as the Holy Book is the word of God, I fail to see how you can spread this nonsense and call it science.'

'My dear woman, I shall answer all questions anon, but first do please let me continue. I have much more to say,' said I, and was pleased to hear a "hear, hear!" from the good doctor and the warden both. The woman did then look as though to speak again, but closed her mouth abruptly and chose to leave. She asked for Miss Jenkins to accompany her, but Miss Jenkins refused and simply called for me to continue. I found her interest most welcoming, and thus did not hesitate to resume.

I spoke for another hour, detailing the reasoning for natural selection to have taken a great part in our own evolution, though a good few people chose to leave before I was spent; finally, I concluded that though such theories contradicted the creation of man and beast as given in the Bible, the evidence for evolution was simply too much for even those not academically minded to ignore. Those left found it in them to applaud, and as my eyes had met the gaze of Miss Jenkins', I did detect but the faintest flicker of a smile.

May 5th, 1882 - Afternoon

The good doctor, Doctor Ravenhill, Miss Jenkins did inform me, visited this afternoon. He has truly an interesting nature, and at great length did we speak of the evolution of man, and of how, during his medical studies, did he have chance to see both the skeleton of man and ape side by side, revealing to him the strong resemblance between the two. He spoke of wishing to attend my next lecture, and informed me that he had written to a dear friend of his to come down and listen also.

'I am glad that you enjoyed it so,' said I. 'I had begun to believe that most thought it not worth attending.'

'My dear man,' replied he, flapping his hand at my words. 'You are educating people on a matter that they have heard only whispers about, and highly negative ones at that. Those who left last night were simply too overwhelmed by the idea to stay to hear another word. The fault was with them, not yourself.'

Miss Jenkins did come over to us just then to announce that luncheon was served in the dining room, but before I could follow Doctor Ravenhill there, she caught my arm for a moment. 'I too enjoyed your lecture last night, Professor, but I feel I must warn you. Do not take lightly the reaction of those who dismissed themselves. Many were angered by your words, and I do not think they will ignore your continued presence here.'

'I understand your concern, Miss Jenkins,' said I.

'But I have simply been sent here to teach. Whether people listen to my lectures or not, it is their own choice. Surely there can be no harm in that?'
She was silent then, and left the Doctor and m alone to enjoy our meal.

May 5ᵗʰ, 1882 - Evening

I gave my second lecture this evening, and I now understand Miss Jenkins's warning. A crowd had gathered outside the doors to shout abuse both at myself and those attending. Fortunately, those who had come to listen chose to ignore the taunts from outside, and so I had followed their example and spoke as though there were no interruptions at all. Once I had concluded, however, I feared for the safety of them all, for the crowd outside had not dispersed. Upon opening the doors, the taunts grew louder and I am certain I heard Madam Clemance, the owner of the hat shop, in their midst, but I could not locate her. Before anyone could provide truly terrible insults, however, Miss Jenkins did appear.
'Enough of this,' said she. All fell silent and departed at once.
'My dear Miss Jenkins,' said I then. 'Truly you must have the respect of all people here, for they obey you without question.'
'Ah, but there you are wrong, Professor. It is not re-

spect for myself; it is respect for my father. If it was not for the thought of him, they would taunt me just as much as they have you.'

'In what profession could your father be in to demand such respect as that?' asked I.

'Be patient, Professor. You may find out on the morrow or if not then, the day after, for he is to travel here to meet you. Did Doctor Ravenhill not speak of this?'

'The friend that Doctor Ravenhill mentioned is your father?'

'Correct, Professor. Now, come along. The night is dark.'

May 6th, 1882

Today I shall take rest from lecturing, to which I hope any animosity towards myself from those who disagree with evolution will die down. The Master had spoken of this task being challenging, for we both knew there would be those who might have trouble accepting such knowledge, but to resort to name calling and outright protesting? Surely that is the pastime of children?

Still, I must not allow myself to be intimidated. I shall go out for a stroll, and if anyone should feel the need to say something objectionable, I shall politely tip my hat and carry on.

May 7*th*, 1882

I was informed this morning that Miss Jenkins' father would be arriving tonight for my last lecture. I do hope that he finds it as interesting as she and Dr Ravenhill have said, for he has travelled far to hear it.

Now I must ready myself, not only for my words, but also for the patience to not cry out to those who would object.

May 8*th*, 1882 - Morning

Oh, but what a to-do was had last night! The great bruise around my eye serves as proof to that, and sorely does it hurt this morning.

Upon making my way to the library, where my lecture was to be held, I was accosted by a large crowd of people, and not only did they say foul things as before, but they did also carry large plaques declaring that I was nothing more than an arrogant blasphemer, who takes pleasure in insulting those of the faith and mocking their beliefs.

I cannot remember all that happened, for I think perhaps that my memory has been affected by the force of the blow I was struck, but I do know that it was Madam

Clemance's husband who struck me first. After that, I am afraid I remember nothing until Doctor Ravenhill and Miss Jenkins arrived, followed by a man of stately manner who did not hesitate to address my attackers. 'Stop this barbaric display!' cried he. 'Are you but heathens, who would attack a man for no reason other than you dislike what he teaches?'

I, then huddled on the ground in the foetal position, heard no reply, or none loud enough to be heard past the ringing that was in my ears. Instead, they did but part aside from me so Doctor Ravenhill could help me up. 'This way, Professor,' said he, and with Miss Jenkins taking hold of my other arm, did lead me slowly to his surgery, which by chance was not far.

He wasted no time in seeking out the many cuts and bruises I had sustained, and cleaned and bandaged them with great efficiency.

'Thank you, sir,' said I most genuinely and stood up.

'What are you doing, Professor?' asked he, his face aghast. 'You must rest now. I shall call a carriage and have it take both you and Miss Jenkins back to the boarding house.'

'Rest? But, good sir, I must give my lecture. Miss Jenkins' father shall be expecting it.'

'My father would never expect you to lecture tonight after seeing such wanton abuse towards you, sir. I expect he shall be occupied until most late. He, himself, shall take confession for all those who have wronged you this night.'

'Confession? He is a man of the church?' asked I, my surprise only too clear even to mine own ears.

'Indeed. A bishop,' said she. 'I was a foundling child, and he found it in his heart to raise me. Now, rest until the carriage arrives. Forget about your lecture, for I shall let you stay two nights more without charge.'

So it is that I have just breakfasted in bed, and now await a visit from the good Bishop who, Miss Jenkins informed me, was still very much interested in hearing me speak. I look forward to his visit, for I must thank him for stopping my attackers last night.

May 8th, 1882 - Evening

The Bishop did come in good time, and a most splendid discussion did we have after I had given my lecture to him. I shall recount it here:

'Sir, I must tell you that you are the only truly devout person thus far who has neither laughed nor grown angry at these theories. I myself had trouble accepting them in my younger days, and I have never followed religious doctrine further than my mother taking me to church every Sunday,' said I to him.

He did smile at that, and replied, 'A theory such as this, to which I believe there is certainly merit, cannot truly shake the faith of anyone, for who is to say that this was not how God's creation of us and the world around us was carried out?

'These people who object must have no ears with which to listen, for they seem to mishear your words. I can find nothing that goes against the Almighty in what you say, and if such people did listen correctly, then they too would see that.'

He stood then and made his pardon for intruding on my rest for so long, and departed from my company to leave me with my thoughts.

I believe that perhaps this proposal of the Master's has found some worth after all. But enough of that, now I must have supper and sleep, for if I am not rested enough to give my last lecture on the morrow, Miss Jenkins has informed me that she will take pay for these extra days after all.

May 13th, 1882

I made my arrival in Norwich today, after extending my stay in King's Lynn for some days more than I'd planned. I do blame myself for falling prey to Miss Jenkins's sensational cooking, though my wallet is now far lighter than I would wish it to be. As such, my lodgings tonight are humble, being the cheapest public house with rooms free that I could find.

My room is adorned only with a bed and washbasin. There is a single outhouse shared with the owners of the establishment and their customers who, due to their manner and general lack of cleanliness, make me unsure of my safety.

Dinner this evening consisted of a simple broth and somewhat stale bread, though I managed to wash it down by brewing up a special blend of tea that Dr Ravenhill gifted me to soothe my nerves. Fortunately, it is a tea served without milk and, boiling some water from the wash jug by the basin by means of a rather ingenious travel stove I had purchased some years ago at an invention convention, complete with kettle, I made a successful brew.

My first lecture here has already been arranged for tomorrow evening, so now I must take to bed if I am to ready myself for it.

May 14*th*, 1882 - Morning

I am always amazed at the early hour some take to drink. The house has barely opened and already every table is full, even the one I now write on while breakfasting. Of course, these men are of a different class than I, and I should be prepared for their ways, but why must this chap insist on leaning over my plate? His odour seems to be making me quite unwell.

Perhaps I shall take a stroll to refresh my nostrils. Oh, how places of lodging can differ depending on the weightiness of your wallet!

May 14th, 1882 - Evening

Whilst exploring the town, I happened to feel for my wallet and, to my disgust, did find it missing. I have reported it to the constabulary, though I fear the constable had his mind more focused on his luncheon than on my words. Though it infuriates me, I must now attend my lecture and so cannot look for the perpetrator myself. My only thought is that it must have been that fragrant fellow from this morning. Oh, how naive could I be?

May 15th, 1882 - Morning

I currently find myself in the cell of Norwich constabulary, my left eye bruised and cut above the eyebrow.

It happened after my lecture had come to an end (which, I may say, went exceedingly well, though there were a few who determined that I should seek guidance from the church to cure me of my delusions). In fact, I was calmly tipping my hat to a particularly appreciative gentleman from the audience when I chanced to see the fellow who I suspected took my wallet while I breakfasted yesterday morning. He had strolled right past the door and, in my anger, I took it upon myself to seek him out and confront him.

The fellow did not take kindly to my accusations and did push me back and, as I lost my balance, my hand flew up and collided with his head. It struck him hard and he fell to the floor, unconscious. A woman near us cried out in alarm and, as fortune would have it, alerted a constable passing us by on his beat.

Before I could explain the situation and have my wallet retrieved, the constable placed me under arrest and took me to the very same station house that I had reported the theft to.

'Constable!' protested I with vigour. 'I know it is your duty to uphold the law, but I promise you that this was an accident. Indeed, had it not been for the fellow pushing me and I losing my balance, then my fist would never have struck his temple.'

'So he pushed you,' said the constable, still leading me rather forcefully down to the cells. 'I suppose that's why you felt it appropriate to sock him one?'

'Sir, please, I already told you what happened. Listen to me, the man stole my wallet earlier and I simply wished to speak to him and ask for it back. There was never any plan to become violent. After all, I am a Professor, not a common ruffian.'

'We get all types in here, *Professor*, and let me tell you they all have the same story,' said he, opening the cell door. 'Now, in you go and be quiet about it. Constable Hitch is on duty down here today, and noisy prisoners tend to try his patience.'

So now it is that I have spent a night in this cell,

with naught but a thin coverlet and, to my distinct distaste, a bedpan so soiled by others that it makes me come over queer just to be near it. All of my belongings, save for this diary, have been taken from me. I *must* find a way to convince them that I am innocent of this crime!

May 15th, 1882 - Evening

I have just come back from being interrogated, a truly frightful experience, I must say. I cannot imagine what those guilty of their accused crimes must feel afterwards, but certainly I feel more drained and weak than I would have thought possible.

After answering a multitude of questions, none of which I felt had anything to do with the matter, I was asked to explain what had happened, though I was interrupted frequently whilst trying to do so.

'So you accidently hit him as you fell, correct?' asked the detective interviewing me. His face was hardened, his voice mechanical and direct.

'Yes, sir, it could not have happened any other way. I am against violence in any form.' I spoke earnestly, yet his stone demeanour did not shift.

'Are you aware that there was a witness?' asked he.

'I know that a lady screamed, but I was not aware that she saw the whole event. If she did, then surely that is proof I am innocent.'

'Had she given the same account as you, it would be. Unfortunately, she was under the impression that you struck out at the man in anger and knocked him unconscious.'

'She is mistaken; perhaps her sight is less than fair?' said I. Truly, it was inconceivable any other way.

The detective ignored me and continued. 'The man in question has also stated that you hit him with intent after accusing him of taking your wallet.'

'He did take my wallet, sir. If he had not, then I would not have confronted him about it.'

'You now admit that you struck him on purpose?' said he, making a note.

'You're twisting my words, sir!' said I, outraged.

'In all the cases that I've investigated, only the persons guilty have reacted in anger when questioned.' He gave me a level gaze and I, taking his meaning, shut my mouth promptly. 'I think that is all for the moment,' said he, gathering his papers.

He signalled to the guards waiting outside and they came and brought me back to this cell. No matter how positive I try to be, things do not look as though they will go in my favour. Perhaps I am cursed with my travels, what with the trouble I had in King's Lynn as well as this.

The hour has grown late and with no lamp to see by, my writing is beginning to blur before my eyes. I think it is time I retired for the night.

May 16ᵗʰ, 1882

To my greatest surprise, I was awoken this morning
by being informed that a visitor had come to see
me. However, I was not to find out who it was until
much later, for the detective had taken in for questioning whoever it was, presumably to find out more
about myself. I hoped that whoever it was knew me
well enough to vouch for my good character, but I
could not even begin to think whom it might be.
The College could not have heard of my misfor-
tunes and I doubted that any of this town cared
enough to see me, unless it was the dark-faced
owner of the public house, come to inform me that
he would keep the room for me no longer.

Before I could get carried away with my thoughts,
however, the guard returned and informed me that
I would be questioned again. He then took me to
the interview room, where the detective was once
again waiting for me.

'I am pleased to see that your temper has cooled.
Perhaps a good sleep in our cosy bed has put you in
high spirits.' He spoke with humour, but there was
none of it in his eyes. Choosing to ignore his ridiculous jibe, I waited for him to continue.

'I have just had a most interesting conversation with
a woman by the name of Kathleen Jenkins.'

'Miss Jenkins? She was here?' said I, astonished.

'You know her, then?' said he.

'Of course I do. Surely she told you that?'

'I did not call you here to discuss what she said.

Why don't you tell me yourself about your relationship to her?'

So it was that I relived my time in King's Lynn to him and, to my great surprise, did he stay quiet until I had finished.

He looked at me for a moment, a slight crease to his brow as though he were calculating something in his mind. 'Are you romantically involved with Miss Jenkins?' said he bluntly.

'Certainly not!' said I, both shocked and affronted at the idea. I am a gentleman, after all. 'I've only been acquainted with her for a week or so. It would be most inappropriate to start up a relationship after so short a time.'

'But you have feelings for her?' said he, with the same delicacy of voice as someone asking me where I might have bought my hat.

Failing to see the relevance of the question, I hesitated, but he cast his strong gaze at me and so I answered. 'I am fond of her, yes. In time, I believe we shall become good friends.'

'I see,' said he and once again summoned the guards to take me away.

I now find myself wondering what Miss Jenkins had wanted of me. How had she come to find me here? And where was the good lady now?

May 17ᵗʰ, 1882 - Morning

I was awoken, early, not by the heavy boots of a constable, but by the gentle yet unmistakable commanding clack of a lady's heeled shoes. Before I could prepare myself for a visit from the fairer sex, I found myself looking into Miss Jenkins' eyes.

'Miss Jenkins!' said I, trying to adjust my shirt collar without her noticing. I hoped also that the stubble on my chin and the unwashed fragrance of my body was not as ungainly as I believed. 'The detective let you down here?'

'He did,' replied she, most calmly. 'There is no need to sharpen your appearance, Professor; I am sure that a night in here wreaks havoc with one's wardrobe.'

'I … yes, indeed, Miss Jenkins. I cannot tell you how wonderful it is to see you, but how did you end up in Norwich?'

'You left one of your books back at the boarding house. I came to give it to you, but when I inquired as to your whereabouts, I heard that you had been accused of assault. So, here I am,' said she, most confidently. 'I have already sent a cable to father explaining the situation. He should be on the next train. I am sure the constabulary will take his words most seriously and free you immediately.'

'Are you sure about this?' asked I uncertainly.

'You are innocent, are you not?'

'I am. I would never strike a man with purpose.'

'Then I am very sure, Professor,' said she, a somewhat metallic strength to her voice. She then left as quickly as she had come and I, entirely bemused by it all, sat in a stupor for several moments before truly comprehending all that she had said. If she and the bishop got their way, then I would be a free man again by the end of the day.

May 17ᵗʰ, 1882 - Evening

The guard on duty disappeared for some moments quite unexpectedly and, when he returned, the detective was with him. To my shame, I was glad to see him looking somewhat harrowed.

'Professor, it seems that you have somehow found yourself a way out of this situation. Once I open this door, you shall be free to go. However,' said he, his usually calculated voice cracking slightly. 'Do not expect the influence of your friends to help you on a second occasion. Even those of a more fortunate social standing are challenged eventually.'

The man could not have been more clear in his meaning, despite how many times I had explained to him that it had all been an accident. Still, he opened the cell door as he had said and I walked out, feeling such relief that it was a wonder I didn't leap down the hall.

As I came out into the station house proper, I was surprised to find both Miss Jenkins and her father waiting for me.

'Professor, it is good to see you looking so well after

such an ordeal,' said the good bishop, looking relieved.

'I must thank you, sir. If you and your daughter had not swayed the detective's judgement, who knows where I would have ended up,' said I. 'I wish I could think of some way to repay you, but I don't believe anything I can offer will be sufficient.'

The good bishop smiled, as did Miss Jenkins. 'I believe there is something,' said she, her cheeks turning a trifle pink. 'I've always wished to travel and now I've found someone to oversee the boarding house whilst I'm away.'

'I'm afraid I don't quite follow,' said I, somewhat puzzled.

'I wish to travel with you,' said she. 'Your funds were stolen from you, were they not? Take me with you and I shall pay for all our needs.'

How could I refuse such an offer from so gracious a lady?

May 18ᵗʰ, 1882

Miss Jenkins and her father stayed overnight with me in Norwich, though they chose to pay for rooms in one of the better hotels in town. My own room, which they also paid for in light of my wallet still not being returned, was glorious compared to the one I had stayed in at the public house and rather a welcome relief from the cell of the station house.

To my greatest delight and fascination, I discovered that there was a fitted bathroom within my quarters. I believe the French call it an *en suite*. How wonderful it is to have my own bath where I may spend as much time as I wish without delaying others! Even at the College my colleagues and I must share.

So it is that I am clean and refreshed this morning, with a full stomach and, once again to the insight of Miss Jenkins, a lecture planned for tonight. First, however, I must cable the College and request more funds for my travels, for despite Miss Jenkins' offer to pay for all our travel expenses, when one considers the costs of running a boarding house, I hardly think it fair. Yet the thought of speaking to the Master does induce within me a sense of apprehension, given that I must explain why the monies I set out with have now been lost.

May 19ᵗʰ, 1882 - Morning

This morning we breakfasted so lavishly that I felt I would never be hungry again. After eating, the good bishop announced that he would be travelling home today and wished myself and Miss Jenkins the best of luck on our journey.

I still have not fully come to terms with the idea of her accompanying me, but I daresay she will be a most lively and knowledgeable companion.

Tonight, I shall give another lecture, once again arranged by Miss Jenkins, and then I shall rest for a day before giving my final one.

It is a good thing that I was not aware of the trouble I would become involved in on this trip, else I would never have considered it. I do hope that there are no other surprises lying in wait.

May 19ᵗʰ, 1882 - Evening

A gentleman came up to me this evening with a most interesting proposal. He asked if I would travel to the Isle of Wight, the island that has taken the favour of Her Majesty and many artists and men of science.

It is said that Charles Darwin began writing 'On the Origin of Species' while he stayed there, so being asked to lecture there felt quite the honour. The gentleman, Mr Edgar Silverston he introduced himself as, stated that he and a few others have formed an organisation of sorts, interested in academic advancement, and that they would be delighted to have me stay with them.

I shall have to speak with Miss Jenkins regarding the matter, but I can foresee no reason as to why she would object. I have heard rumours that the island itself is most beautiful, a sight that everyone should see.

May 20ᵗʰ, 1882

To my delight, Miss Jenkins has agreed to travel with me to the Isle of Wight. As she believes it will be somewhat of an extended stay, she has asked me to accompany her shopping so she may buy more suitable clothes. As I found earlier, she knew far more about the famed isle than I, and did tell me that recreational walking and horseback riding are activities enjoyed by many there, as well as sailing and swimming. I believe our stay there shall be most precious, though how much time I shall have for such things is yet to be determined.

May 21ˢᵗ, 1882

Mr Silverston recently sent word that he and his colleagues would not be expecting me on the fair isle for several weeks, so it is that I have planned out our journey so that I may stop in several towns to lecture and, if time allows, even London. The Master did say to travel as much as I could, and as he so graciously granted the extra monies I asked for, I see no reason to waste the opportunity. Tomorrow Miss Jenkins and I shall set off for Lowestoft and, from there, to Ipswich. I believe that she is more excited than I, for still I am wary of further incidents. Nevertheless, I shall leave her unawares of my fears, for it is a sad thing to mottle another's experiences with such gloom.

May 23rd, 1882

Miss Jenkins and I are currently on board the train to Ipswich, having given just the single lecture in Lowestoft. I would have stayed longer, for though there were the usual objections, the audience in general seemed most obliging and some even stayed for a short while afterwards to discuss it further. One man, a baker I believe, even stated that he had always felt that humans were connected in some way with animals, but had never managed to figure out how. Darwin's theories had given him peace of mind at last.

As much as I delighted in the place however, it seemed that Miss Jenkins did not. I often thought about asking her why, but one must not pry into a lady's business, despite how much she has been prying into my own of late. I must say that though we have only been in each other's company for a few days, she already knows all that happened in my rather simple childhood and all that transpired at the College before I set out.

I cannot help but wonder what she thinks of me, nor can I stop pondering whether our friendship will become anything more than just that. Are such thoughts really so improper?

May 26th, 1882

Oh, but how busy we have been these last few days. We stayed in Ipswich for two nights and, due to Miss Jenkins' insight to cable forward from Lowestoft to make arrangements, I gave lectures on both evenings. From there, we caught the train to London which, upon our arrival, Miss Jenkins declared it the filthiest place she had ever been. I was inclined to agree with her.

So many bodies in so small a space began to make me feel quite unwell, but my nausea subsided once we were in the carriage taking us to the hotel that Miss Jenkins made a point of selecting herself. Truly, she is both a woman of fine taste and sensible mind, for even in such a place, our rooms are comfortable and practical, yet incur no great fee.

Tonight, I shall give my first and only lecture here, for to stay any longer would turn any man crazed. Perhaps that is why so many here turn to crime.

May 27th, 1882

We arrived in Brighton yesterday, a most refreshing town. I already feel that the murk of London is being cleared from my being by the fresh, salted air. This is the last place in which we shall stop before making our way to the Isle of Wight and, by Jove, I intend to enjoy it.

The swelling of the waves upon the shores is certainly most calming and compels me to ponder the vast density of life within the ocean depths. Alas, Miss Jenkins believes the best way to experience the ocean is by swimming in it and, due to my shameful confession of never having done so before, she has promised to teach me the basics. What a modern woman she is!

June 1st, 1882

Miss Jenkins and I finally arrived on the Isle of Wight this evening, having taken the train to Portsmouth Harbour and boarding the ferry (a capable paddle steamer named *PS Victoria*, introduced to the fleet just last year, the good ticket master did explain to us). The sea was remarkably calm and so the crossing was pleasant, though Miss Jenkins came over somewhat faint. However, her recovery was quick once we disembarked and soon we took a train to the village of Bembridge, where Mr Silverston was to meet us.

We made good time and found a carriage awaiting us, though no sign of Mr Silverston himself. When questioning the driver about it, he simply stated that he had been instructed to bring one Professor Marcellus Kingston and one Miss Kathleen Jenkins to Heathshield House, where we would be boarding for the duration of our stay.

Miss Jenkins advised me not to pursue the matter, sure that all would be sorted upon our arrival and, indeed, it was.

Heathshield House turned out to be a rather large and important looking building on the outskirts of the village and housed ten rooms, not including the dining room and conference room. I found it delightful, for upon each wall were great shelves full of books on modern science, art and literature. Had Miss Jenkins not delicately but forcefully taken my arm and led me over to where Mr Silverston had just then made his appearance, I would have marvelled there for hours.

'I am terribly sorry I missed you at the station,' began he. 'I'm afraid my work caught up with me and stole my time. I do hope you were not offended?'

'Not at all, Mr Silverston. We thought something of that nature had occurred,' said Miss Jenkins smoothly. I gave a nod, my eyes still tracing the titles of the volumes on the wall behind him.

'Ah,' said he, realising that he had caught my glance. 'Do please feel free to read anything you wish. I believe that aside from your lectures on evolution, you teach geology, do you not?'

'You are correct, sir,' replied I, impressed that he knew so much of me.

'Then I believe you shall find the books I had placed in your room most interesting. As for yourself, Miss Jenkins, I wondered whether you would like the literary works of the Brontë sisters. Have you heard of them?' asked he.

'I have, though sadly I have yet to read any. I must say, Mr Silverston, your courtesy knows no bounds,' said she. Such flattery!

We spoke for only a few moments longer before we were shown to our rooms, as the hour was getting late and we needed to refresh ourselves and change before heading down to the dining room.

June 2nd, 1882

I cannot express how inspiring our conversation was last evening. Seated at the table were several others, each of them boarding here themselves. Clockwise around the table, their names were: Dr James Haversmith, who runs a clinic for those having suffered intense trauma either from war or other means; Mr Edward Stonefair, chief librarian for the island; Miss Elizabeth Telmar, an archaeologist recently back from an excavation in Egypt; Professor Albert Hues, a lecturer on mathematics and, of course, Mr Silverston himself, who owns a company that deals in the manufacture of dry plates for use with a camera, and thus dabbles in photography himself.

Needless to say, we had much to talk about and, to my delight, Miss Jenkins took full part in the conversation too, frequently questioning each on their area of expertise and revealing to everyone her own experiences with photography, to which I confess I am somewhat in awe. I feel that she may be one of those exemplary people who do well at anything they put their minds to.

Today, Mr Silverston has arranged a tour of the island for us so that we may feel more settled and, I believe, to provide opportunity to arrange suitable venues for the lectures I shall give during my stay. Ah, there is a call at the door even now to say that our carriage is ready. I feel it shall be a most educational outing.

June 10th, 1882

The week has passed quickly and I truly feel as settled here as ever I was in Cambridge. I have given lectures in Ryde (the charming town where the *PS Victoria* came to port) and Newport, the centremost town on the island. The response to both was exceedingly positive, something which I hope will be prevalent for all my lectures here.

I have also, with thanks to Mr Silverston's recommendations, been invited to take part in some geological fieldwork, something that I have missed sorely since becoming a Fellow of the College. I believe the site location is named Alum Bay which, as Mr Silverston explained, is famous for its colourful sandstone. Miss Jenkins is to accompany me and, I am told, has been given full use of Mr Silverston's best camera for the occasion. I admit I am anxious to see her abilities first-hand.

June 15th, 1882

After our fieldwork this morning at Alum Bay, which has left me rather invigorated, I am glad to say it shall continue for another few days yet. Mr Silverston and Miss Telmar have invited us to an evening lecture. It is to be on the archaeological findings on the island and I believe there will be various bones and fossils on display, which I find most interesting.

I do believe that Miss Telmar has organised the event, being something of a close friend of the archaeologist speaking there. I never before dreamed that this small island could have such a fascinating history; it is enough to make me wish to extend our stay here. Having spoken just recently to Miss Jenkins on the matter, it is clear that she feels the same way.

There is but one thing which concerns me, and that is the appearance of a number of unfortunate women strolling around each evening. I can only conclude that they are such, as no respectable woman would seek fresh air so late at night. However, they never come close to the house, nor cause trouble, so perhaps my concerns are of no consequence. I certainly haven't felt it necessary to inform Miss Jenkins of the matter, and would dearly wish to keep it such.

June 17ᵗʰ, 1882 - Night

I have just been awoken by someone running about the corridor. Upon checking to see who it was, I found no one at all and so resolved that it had been my imagination. Still, I cannot but feel that there is something amiss. I would not have thought a burglar would be so loud, nor have the opportunity to break in, for the butler keeps all doors and windows under tight lock and key, and has a room situated such that the slightest noise would wake him.

June 18ᵗʰ, 1882

Due to my interrupted sleep in the night, I find I am somewhat weary this morning. I asked Miss Jenkins, having her room situated next to mine, if she had heard any disturbances, but she informed me that she had not and indeed looked far more well rested than I.

As we breakfasted, the other members of our company gradually appeared, but they too had heard nothing. Perhaps it had been a figment of my imagination.

I shall put the matter from my mind, for I have a lecture this evening and must make preparations. Miss Jenkins has been invited out for lunch, so I am free to busy myself with my reading and presentation.

June 20th, 1882 - Morning

I fear I am losing my senses, for now I have been disturbed three nights in a row, yet no one else has heard a sound. I find it sorely tempting to consult with Dr Haversmith on the matter, but I am somewhat reluctant to admit that I am hearing things. Perhaps I shall write to Dr Ravenhill instead; somehow, I feel any diagnosis from him may be easier to take.

June 20th, 1882 - Midnight

Again, I heard the sound of heavy footsteps past my door, though I refused to look this time. Whether it is my imagination or a cruel prank, I am tired of it. I must sleep and regain at least some sense of self.

June 21st, 1882

The events of this day have been such that it is a wonder I am not so shaken as to lose the use of my hand. Once again, I find myself in the cell of the local constabulary, though it is not simply a case of assault this time.

Somehow, I find myself accused of murder, and murder most foul at that.

I had woken this morning to the sound of panic throughout the house and, upon opening my door to see what the commotion was, I found a slender limp form before me, with blood all upon the carpet and walls.

I admit that at first I froze, thinking that this delicate female form could only be that of Miss Jenkins, but then I noticed the dirt upon the poor woman's face and hands, and the tattered state of her attire. No, she was one of the unfortunates that I had seen wandering late at night about the town. Yet how had she ended up inside, and murdered so brutally to boot?

Miss Jenkins had come out of her room then and, seeing the sight before me, screamed more shrilly than I had thought possible, alerting the rest of the household.

'My gosh!' ejaculated Mr Silverston, also happening upon the sight. 'We knew that someone had broken in, but this? What in heaven's happened?'

I told them all what I had heard during the night, but that I had seen nothing.

'Do we know who she is?' asked Mr Stonefair.

'Yes,' replied I. 'She was a lady of the night. I used to see her from my window during my hours of study.'

'A lady of the night?' said Miss Jenkins. 'You mean to say …?'

'You must be mistaken, sir,' said Mr Silverston. 'We have no such women around here.'

I chose not to argue, seeing that it would only intensify the situation. 'We must contact the constabulary. They shall surely solve this mystery,' said I, my words sounding more sure than thoughts in my mind.

However, after arriving and having questioned us all, the constable and the detective (this one older and with a look of understanding that his counterpart in Norwich could never have) took me in for questioning.

'Professor, though I myself cannot imagine it, we received notification from a stationhouse up in Norwich that a man fitting your name and description had recently committed a crime and may seek to do the same here. The detective there was most adamant about it and, given the circumstances, I have no choice but to take you in.'

I could see the man was most upset at having to do so, but it angered me all the same. I swore heartily under my breath at the detective in Norwich. Why couldn't the man understand that I had done nothing wrong?

I was questioned for a full hour, yet they believed my answers to be inconclusive and so decided to keep me in overnight while the investigation gets underway.

June 22nd, 1882

As expected, due to lack of evidence, I was released and allowed to go back to Heathshield House. Upon my arrival, I found the house still aflutter with activity and I was submitted to more questioning by everyone, all except for Miss Jenkins, who was nowhere in sight.

Making my excuses and promising to tell all that had happened later, I went to her room to see if she was there. As I walked past my own room, I noticed that effort had been made to remove the bloodstains from the carpet, but a large amount remained. I hope that it will be removed swiftly, for I do not much fancy stepping over it each morning.

I knocked on Miss Jenkins' door and she answered from within, granting me entry.

'Marcellus!' said she, her forwardness taking me

aback slightly. 'I was truly worried that they might charge you this time.'

'Thank you for your concern, Miss Jenkins. It delights my heart greatly, but you need not be worried, there was no evidence against me. They had no option but to release me.'

She smiled then, standing from her seat at the desk and coming over to me. 'I am glad,' said she, taking my hand.

'Miss Jenkins, I hardly think that is appropriate,' declared I, but my voice faltered as her gaze hardened.

'Marcellus, I have known you for a while now. Please let us not always be so formal with each other.' Her gaze did soften and I felt my palms moisten slightly and my throat grow dry.

'Very well, then … Kathleen,' said I, and found myself embracing her. She let me do so for a moment, but then broke away.

'Well, then,' said she, a slight blush creeping across her cheeks. 'What shall we do?'

'Do? I'm afraid I don't quite follow.'

'Are you not curious as to how the body of a strange woman ended up outside your door?'

I admit I had not been expecting such a question and so stood dumbstruck for a moment. 'I suppose I am, yes.'

'Then we shall have to find out what happened. Tell me again about those noises you have been hearing at night.'

I did so and she listened intently. 'It does not give us much to pursue, I admit,' said she after. 'But perhaps we may speak with the butler and hear his thoughts on the matter. Let us find him this evening, after dinner.'

Thus, it is that our curious investigation begins.

June 23rd, 1882

Our conversation last night with the butler, Mr Jessops, was most interesting and revealed him to be a man of utmost dependency and vigour.

We spoke at length of his nightly routine, which was far more strict than I would ever have guessed. As soon as all the occupants have retired for the evening, Mr Jessops locks the main door and all side doors, as well as all the windows, aside from those in each individual's room. He then sets up a series of wires, each linked to one of the windows or doors, all of which are fixed to bells in his room that, when triggered, let him know that someone is attempting to break in and at which point.

I must say, that such an alarm system sounds most efficient and I advised Mr Jessops to put it forward at an invention convention, though he did quickly put the thought from his mind, saying that he had no ambitions to do so.

Furthermore, his preparations do not end there, for he did say that he wakes three times each night to patrol the corridors, though on that particular night he fell rather ill and had to ask Mr Silverston to take up the task for him.

'So,' said Kathleen. (Oh, how strange it is to call her by her first name!) 'It was Mr Silverston who patrolled that night?'

'Yes, madam, it was. However, I have no doubt that he performed the duty as well, if not better, than I,' answered he.

'I must enquire,' said I. 'What can you tell us about the women I've been seeing from my window during the night?'

'Well, Professor, your impression of them was correct the first time. They were unfortunates, and certainly unfavourable by anyone decent. Mr Silverston has tried many times to have them removed by the constabulary, but as they have never been caught in the, ah, *act* …' explained he, coughing delicately as he looked at Kathleen.

'There's no need to be polite, Mr Jessops. I know full well what sorts of things go on with these women. Still, if Mr Silverston knows who they are, why did he so clearly deny that there were any such persons near here when we found the body?' said Kathleen.

Mr Jessops shrugged, a most alien movement for a man of such discipline. 'I can only suppose that he now finds it easier to deny the situation than to acknowledge it.'

He had told us all he knew, so we could only leave

him to his duties and speculate on the matter ourselves.

Kathleen suggested that we ask Dr Haversmith if he might procure the details of the post mortem so that we could piece this puzzle together better. I feel it is a good idea, though whether he is privy to that information I do not know.

In the end, it was decided that I speak to him alone while Kathleen speaks with Mr Silverston about taking over Mr Jessops' patrol on that night.

Now that I have had time to consider the matter properly, I wonder that no one is in fear of having a murderer amongst us. After all, regardless of who the woman was, she was murdered here. It would have been hard for her to come in unnoticed, let alone having her murderer come in too.

June 26th, 1882

Kathleen has yet to speak with Mr Silverston, as he seems to have been unusually busy these past few days. Even at mealtimes, he is the last to arrive and the first to leave. I must wonder if he is avoiding us all but, of course, the press have been questioning him most fiercely of late.

I had much more success with Dr Haversmith and, to my delight, he told me that his good standing in the medical field had allowed him to procure the coroner's report. Aside from the rather indelicate details of her wounds, the woman was found to be with child. The coroner had also found a handkerchief embroidered with the letters E.S., though whether the initials were hers or another's is to be determined.

June 27th, 1882

Kathleen and I have been discussing the matter in detail and, no sooner had I mentioned the handkerchief than she asked as to how well made it was. At first I thought it was just her curiosity as a woman, but she persisted and so we went to speak with Dr Haversmith again to see if he had such a detail. To my great surprise, he did and it was found that the handkerchief had been made of embroidered silk, something that, as Kathleen did point out, a woman of such standing would have found difficult to come by.

'Then we can only assume that it was given to her by someone else, a person with the initials of E.S. and with a rather high social standing. Perhaps the owner of a dry plate company,' said she, most seriously.

I admit that the initials of E.S. match with that of Mr Silverston, but her directness was still a shock. 'But Kathleen, what would Mr Silverston want with such a woman?' asked I, bemused.

'I would have thought the answer to that was most

obvious, Marcellus. My guess would be that the child was his.'

'Oh, come now, Kathleen. With a woman of her profession, the child could have been anybody's,' said I.

'Yes, but I'm afraid the handkerchief and the very fact that you said you saw her close to this house every night lead me to believe that, even if the child wasn't truly his, the woman was convinced it was,' explained she. 'Perhaps she tried to convince him to marry her, or at least see to the child's future. Whatever the reason, Mr Silverston clearly could not accept it.'

'Do you really believe he could have done it? And so horribly, at that?'

'Yes. I believe that if you push a man into a corner, he will do almost anything to escape. Remember, Marcellus, that my father is a bishop. When I was a child I used to help clean the church, and there were times when I was close to the confessional that I heard all manner of things, some not so far from this.'

'But why kill her outside my door? And what were the noises during the night for?' asked I, still puzzled by it all, but nonetheless awed by her power of deduction.

'To that I have no answer. We must speak with him at once.'

To our great annoyance, we found that Mr Silverston was on an outing and had not disclosed the location to anyone. Now all we can do is wait for his return.

June 28th, 1882

Kathleen and I cornered Mr Silverston after we had breakfasted this morning. We had been determined not to let him escape us and, as he made his way back to his room to collect his case and jacket, we followed and met him there.

'Mr Silverston, may we have a moment?' asked I, but Kathleen cut across me.

'Edgar Silverston,' said she. 'Your initials would be E.S., would they not? A handkerchief with those same initials was found on the body of the woman who was murdered here.'

Her eyes met his and I noticed his face did pale considerably. However, he recovered rather speedily and had I not been paying close attention, I would have missed it.

'My dear Miss Jenkins,' said he, sadly. 'I'm afraid I have no idea what you are talking about. Are you trying to say that somehow this woman possessed one of my handkerchiefs?'

'Yes indeed, sir. Furthermore, I believe that you gave it to her as a token of affection,' replied she.

'My good woman, what a fantastical imagination you have! Tell me, do you have proof to support this *outlandish* idea?' His response was so petulant that it convinced me Kathleen was correct in her thinking.

'We have proof that she was with child, Mr Silverston. We now also have proof that you own several silk handkerchiefs with the initials E.S. upon them which, according to the description, match the one in the woman's possession,' explained I after a swift nod from Kathleen who, in her brilliance while Mr Silverston's attention was on myself, had discreetly opened the drawer containing such handkerchiefs (the knowledge of which came from her observation of Mr Jessops as he put away his master's laundry yesterday afternoon).

Mr Silverston saw her and his face grew red and brutish. 'You prying floozy! How dare you accuse me of consorting with that doxy!' spat he and began to advance on her, yet before I had time to bar his path for fear of her safety, the door swung open and Mr Jessops stood there, his face a cloud of disgust.

'That is enough, sir!' said he to Mr Silverston, dropping all politeness of manner in the heat of his anger. 'I have just contacted the constabulary, who informed me they would set out immediately. They are coming to place you under arrest.'

'Jessops, you fool! Do not tell me that you, my own butler, are convinced by the charade this woman and the Professor concocted together to incriminate me?' demanded Mr Silverston.

'Sir, I have known you for more than ten years. You

would never become so enraged at such accusations if they had not a shred of truth, yet here you are, about to raise your hand to strike a lady. That is all the proof I need to know their accusations are just,' said Mr Jessops, his voice hard.

The detective and two constables arrived a short while later, after Mr Jessops had escorted Mr Silverston downstairs and stood guard over him to make sure he did not try to leave the premises.
The constables took hold of Mr Silverston while the detective took a short statement from Kathleen, Mr Jessops and myself. When he was satisfied, he and the constables left with Mr Silverston for the stationhouse.
Afterwards, Mr Jessops kindly served Kathleen and I tea and scones to help calm both our nerves. We invited him to sit with us and, with thanks, he did so. It was then that Kathleen and I learned that he had been listening in on our conversation with Mr Silverston and as soon as he heard the initials on the handkerchief, he guessed what had happened just as we and immediately cabled the constabulary. Now we must wait for the result, but in my mind, I have no doubt now of his guilt. I admit I wonder what Mr Jessops' plans are if Mr Silverston *is* convicted, for his role as butler at Heathshield House will surely be at an end. Still, a man so capable as he should find no problem securing another position; at least, that is my hope.

June 29th, 1882

The detective visited us late this morning, stating that after vigorous questioning, Mr Silverston had confessed. He had been the woman's client for some years, but had found himself somewhat attached to her. However, as Kathleen had surmised, she had strongly believed the child to have been his and, afraid that her words were true, that was something he could not face. It would have sullied his name and reputation, something he could ill afford.

He had planned the deed weeks before and, on the night, had drugged Mr Jessops with the intent to replace the butler on the nightly patrol of the corridors. Once the household was asleep, he had dismantled the alarm bells and let her in, after which he struck her unconscious and then murdered her outside my door.

Our company was shocked, not having known the goings on of the past few days, but Kathleen, Mr Jessops and I all felt relief that the case had been solved and the murderer known, yet it is still hard to think that a man of such promise and status can sink so low.

'What of those noises I heard during the night?' said I. 'Did he speak of those?'

'He did, sir, yes. It was his plan to implicate you as the perpetrator, seeing as you're a stranger here and thus the most suspicious. Your recent involvement with the constabulary also helped solidify his plan, I believe. The noises were his attempt to make you believe that you were losing your senses to further sully your credibility. However, he did not reckon that one of my constables should read your journal and so know that you were a man of sound mind.'

'You read my journal?' asked I, stunned.

'I did,' said he. 'I must admit that you have some unfortunate luck, sir. I hope that your future travels shall go without incident.'

'Detective,' said I, feeling suddenly weary. 'I do not believe my travels will continue after this. It appears that an adventurous life is not for me. No, I shall return home to Cambridge and continue to lecture there on geology only.'

To my surprise, Kathleen stood up at this. 'Marcellus, you cannot mean that! You promised to travel together with me, giving lectures on Darwin's theories. I cannot let you break it simply because of a little misfortune.'

She spoke so passionately that I felt truly ashamed of myself. If she has the courage to keep by my side, then how could I refuse?

September 24th, 1896
Dearest Uncle,

I cannot tell you how fascinating the pages you sent me were.

It is clear now what my father has always told me about making mistakes—that it is what we do afterwards that matters, rather than the mistake itself. Had Mr Silverston taken responsibility for that unfortunate woman, then her life would have been spared and the whole situation different. Alas, it seems not everyone makes the correct choices in life.
I also believe I have a much greater understanding as to why you are always so obedient to Aunt Kathleen's wishes, though I can see that your confidence in your self has not improved much over the years!

Mother and I hope to visit near Christmas.
Until then,
Thomas

Flight in the Dark

MYO LOOKED AT HIS BROTHER, Tis, as they hung upside down in the hollow of their tree. Tis was solemn, unmoving, as if he had no concern other than breathing.

But Myo was restless. He could taste the change in the air; the sun was sinking and soon they would fly out, across the foliage to the lake, where they would feast on flies and gnats for most of the night.

He shifted his feet, making his head sway in the air. Hunger gnawed at him; he could already smell the insects flying about. However, hunting before it was truly dark was dangerous. That's how their mother had lost her life when they'd been just infants.

One moment she'd been pursuing prey using her echo, the next a bird, quick and sharp, swooped down and snatched her away, never to be seen again.

Fortunately, their cousins roosted with them and raised the brothers from then onwards. They learnt how to fly and hunt in a group, and had done so ever since.

Myo's stomach growled. 'I can't stand it any longer, brother,' he complained.

'Quiet. We must wait for the call as always. It won't be long now,' Tis replied, agitation in his voice.

Myo sulked in silence. Tis had always been the boss of him, a side effect of being five seconds older. Myo was still the swiftest though, so he thought that should have balanced things out.

A vibration cut through the air, intense and widespread. That was the signal. Now they could fly.

Spreading their large leathery wings, they let go of the tree and zoomed out of the hollow, gliding on the air. Myo caught an insect before his body fully left the tree's reach; he swallowed it whole, grinning with satisfaction.

'Don't go flying off on your own, Myo,' Tis warned before Myo could be distracted by more prey. 'We've got to meet up with the others so we can hunt together by the lake.'

Myo rolled his eyes, but did as he was told.

A moment later, he and Tis joined up with the

group and as one large mass of black wings they glided into the night, synchronising their calls so they could locate all the insects in the area.

There was only one problem, one that they had never encountered before. There *were* no insects. At least, not enough for them all to feed on.

Confused, the formation began to break up. Tis took charge and called for them to keep going until they reached the lake. Perhaps the insects were lurking far out on the water's surface?

The group acknowledged his call and re-banded, but when they got to the lake, they fared no better. To their dismay, the water level had dropped, and ash and soil filled it instead. It harboured even fewer insects than the rest of the forest. It didn't make sense. Only the night before, the lake had been full, and the air swarming with moths, flies and beetles that the group had feasted on with hundreds more to spare.

'This is no good. We can't hunt like this,' Tis said, turning to Myo. But Myo wasn't there. Tis looked up and felt the air drafts from Myo's wings as the younger bat flew higher and higher. 'Myo, where do you think you're going?'

Cursing, Tis flew after him, going against his instincts and separating from the group. As they broke through the forest's canopy, Tis stopped.

Before him, spread across the landscape, were not the miles of trees he'd expected to see in the moon's luminous light, but a land that was flat and grey.

He couldn't see any other creatures flying about, or feel them when he sent out his locating calls. There were no calls, no smells, not even the fresh scent of earth and tree sap that usually filled the area on hot, sticky nights.

There was nothing. The land was dead.

'What's happened here, Tis?' Myo asked, swooping in beside his brother. They landed on the top of the nearest tree, looking out across the wasteland.

Tis couldn't reply, shock had taken hold of him completely. Myo sat beside him in silence, waiting. Eventually, he gave up and flew back down through the trees to find the group.

He found them in chaos. Their formation was completely broken and blind panic had taken over. They were so desperate to find food that they flitted back and forth in every direction possible, chittering anxiously. The noise was overwhelming.

Myo latched on to a nearby tree, thinking what to do. He could try to order them, but he didn't have the authority in his call that Tis did. In their state, it would be impossible for him to calm them.

Nervously, he adjusted his focus away from his fellows. Despite there being no sign of life in the area that he and Tis had looked out on, there was still plenty down near the lake. He backed up against the tree's great trunk, merging with the moss growing on it.

There was a rustle above him, and before he could even let out a warning, an owl ten times his size swooped down onto the scene and seized one of his cousins in mid-air. Other owls followed suit, the confusion of the bats making for an easy meal.

Horror and shame gripped Myo as he watched his friends and family picked off one by one. But what could he, the bat everyone thought was an idiot, do to try and save them?

In the state they were in, he doubted Tis could even force them to obey. So he stayed hidden, shaking amongst the leaves, hoping that Tis would remain safe above the canopy until it was all over.

———

Tis called for Myo desperately. He couldn't find any trace of the group—it was as if they'd all disappeared somewhere.

A muffled call sounded back, and Tis turned to see Myo crawl out from the moss of a tree.

'Tis!' Myo cried, flying to him. 'Are you alright? You're not hurt?'

'Hurt? Why would I be hurt?' Tis asked, worried by the desperate look in his brother's eyes.

'When I flew back down here, the group was in a mess. They were flying out of formation and going everywhere. Then *they* came, swooping down on everybody. Nobody had a chance. They took everyone,' Myo sobbed.

'Who's "they"?' Tis asked, though in his heart he knew. 'The ones who took mother?'

Myo only nodded in reply. Tis felt the strength leave his wings and had to grip a nearby branch for support. His whole family, aside from Myo, had been wiped out in just a few moments? How was it possible?

The crack of dry wood from a dead tree split the calm of the night.

'Myo, we've got to get out of here,' Tis said quietly. He could feel eyes on them, waiting to attack.

Another branch snapped. They looked at each other, both sensing a mutual plan forming. They sidled around to the other side of the tree, and as soon as they got there, they took flight, zigzagging through the trees. Tis was in the lead, guiding Myo as he tracked the wings of a large bird behind them.

The sound grew closer and the trees became dense, making them hard to navigate.

Tis had no choice. 'Myo, we've got to go up!'

Without waiting for a reply, Tis tilted sharply, bulleting upwards and out above the canopy again.

There was a screech behind him, but when he turned, all he saw was Myo breaking through the treetops.

'We did it,' Myo said breathlessly. 'It couldn't get through the canopy, the leaves are too thick.'

Loud thrashings echoed below them. 'I don't

think we should wait around. That thing is far more powerful than we are; there's no telling when it will break through,' Tis declared.

They flew on, not looking back, until the sun began to rise. By then, they'd travelled further than ever had before, and were in unfamiliar territory.

Just as the first rays of sunlight reached them, they dived back below the canopy and clung to a gnarled, woody vine. 'We'll have to rest here for now,' Tis said, thankful to finally fold his wings. 'At nightfall, we'll look for a proper place to roost. Somewhere safe.'

Myo could barely nod his agreement; within moments, he was asleep.

The next thing he knew, Tis was shaking him awake. He opened his eyes and froze. A green, scaled face was staring at him, flicking a forked tongue in and out. 'What is it?' he whispered to Tis.

Tis swallowed. 'A snake.'

'And do snakes … eat bats?' Myo asked, shaking as the thing slithered closer.

'Yes—fly!' Tis screamed, launching himself from the vine, grabbing hold of Myo with his bony feet. The snake struck as they did so, missing Myo by mere centimetres.

For the first few moments, they fell, unable to get any lift, but then Tis' wings came back to life and he opened them out fully, catching the air. Myo released his own wings and they darted away, almost careering into each other as the sun caught their eyes.

They flew for the rest of the day, stopping to rest for no more than a few minutes at a time, seeking out a place to roost that was free from birds of prey *and* snakes.

By the time the sun began to sink, they had only found one tree they could roost in and, even more exhausted than before, they crawled inside its small hollow.

———

'Hey!'

Tis and Myo opened their eyes. Another bat hung inches away. It was twice their size, and had an elongated nose. 'What are you two brats doing in my tree?' he asked, sneering at them.

Tis swallowed, but Myo spoke first. 'Your tree? What makes it yours?' he asked. 'We found it empty. If it's yours, then why weren't you in it?'

'What impudence!' the bat spluttered. 'I was out hunting, you idiot. Now, get out so I can have some rest!'

'No—' Myo began, but Tis broke in.

'What my brother meant to say, sir, is that we recently lost our family and our home, and now we have nowhere to go. Please, let us rest here for a few hours so we can regain our strength.'

The bat stared at him. 'Alright, but *only* for a few hours. After that, you must leave.'

'Thank you, sir,' Tis said respectfully, holding his wing across Myo so that he couldn't say anything.

The bat made to turn his back on them, but paused instead. 'If you really are in trouble like you say ... then I know where you might find some others of your kind,' he muttered.

'Really?' Myo asked, pushing Tis' wing out of the way. 'Where?'

'You're full of questions, aren't you? Leave me in peace for a while and I might consider showing you. Go to sleep.'

Myo pouted, but he didn't antagonise the old bat further.

———

A few hours later, the old bat woke them with a gruff chitter. 'Are you two coming?' he demanded and, without waiting, took flight.

Still weary, Myo and Tis followed him as he darted through the air, every now and then catching an insect and swallowing it with delight.

The brothers did the same, relishing the amount of insects swarming about in the night.

The death that had crept up on the forest where they used to live obviously hadn't ventured here.

After only a short distance, they broke through a

thick bush, and on the other side was a collection of bats hunting as a team. Tis and Myo cried at the sight. One of the group flew over to inspect them.

'Booga, what brings you to these parts?' she asked, talking to the old bat.

'These two brats are survivors of a predator attack on their group. They are the only ones who made it, and now they have no family and nowhere to roost,' Booga replied, not unkindly.

'I see. In that case, boys, what are your names?' she asked.

'I'm Tis, and this is my brother, Myo,' Tis answered.

'I see. I am called Hea, and I lead this group. Tell me, are you any good at hunting in within a team?'

'Of course we are,' Myo replied, his cockiness clear in his voice.

Hea smiled. 'In that case, we welcome you. Come and hunt with us, and we will find you shelter.' She turned to Booga, who was just about to leave. 'Thank you for bringing them to us. I hope you know that you are welcome to join us too, if you wish.'

'Nonsense, I don't need a group to help me hunt. I'm fine on my own. Besides, we're two different species.'

He flew off, back though the bushes. Hea sighed. 'That bat never learns.'

'What do you mean?' Tis asked her, curious.

'He lost his family too, by a threat far greater than the normal predators we face. He searched many years for others of his kind, but now he is the only one left. Anyway, enough of this talk, we have work to do,' she said, and led them into the group to meet their new family.

Sanguine

THE SUN IS SETTING, spreading gold onto the walls of the room. I stand up the stool by my desk and walk to the window, looking out at the grounds below.

I see them outside, enjoying a game of catch, my husband watching over attentively. They are so young, so full of life.

The clock strikes six, signalling the need to dress for dinner. I choose the green velvet gown; the weight of it makes me feel strong and the movement it has as I walk ripples with femininity.

As I descend the stairs, a tremor runs through me, weakening my grip on the rail and causing nausea to rise so swiftly, I have no choice but to pause. I calm myself as I've done many times before; I cannot appear frail in front of them. I must not.

When I enter the dining room I find them all seated and waiting, my girls in identical yellow frocks, and my husband in his usual dining jacket.

'Mother, you're late,' Liza says as I take my seat. It's true; the clock shows thirty-five minutes past six. Dinner is strictly at six thirty. I have never been late before.

'I'm sorry my darlings, but I had the most *awful* time pinning my hair. It just *wouldn't* stay,' I say dramatically, casting the back of my hand to my forehead. They both giggle. 'I hope you're not terribly cross with me.'

'We could never be cross with you, Mother,' Freya says.

I smile warmly, but notice the crease on my husband's brow. He understands exactly why I was late.

'Well, now we're all here, would you care to bring out the first course, Henry?' he asks our butler. Henry dashes off to fetch a delicious starter of shrimp in a delicate sauce.

I savour each mouthful.

When the meal is over, I see the girls to bed, and then meet my husband in the gardens. We walk together, arm in arm, and I revel in the warmth of him. The air is particularly fresh, and the stars sparkle brightly. It's a perfect evening.

We come upon a table set with red wine, and he lights a perfumed candle. He knows how much I love them.

'Is it ready?' I ask.

'Yes,' he replies, handing me a glass and filling it halfway with the sweet-smelling wine. 'Are you sure you want to?'

'More than you can know, my love.' I take the glass to my lips and swallow, watching the single tear roll down his cheek.

Mould in the Jam Jar

SALLY KNEW THE PATH, her memory hadn't failed her. The sweet, slightly sickly scent of decaying leaves and pollen met her with each step as she made her way along the woods' obscure pathway. Behind, her sisters were running to catch up, their voices breathless as they called for her to slow down, Audrey swearing at the top of her lungs with each sentence.

Sally heard them, but her feet wouldn't obey. They kept on, tread after tread as if the whole world would stop existing if she halted for even a moment.

The woods truly were beautiful at this time of year. She'd missed them. The overhanging limbs of the oaks that she had to duck under, purple thistles reaching up to her thigh and everywhere, butterflies.

It is said that butterflies are the souls of the dead watching over us.

If that were true, they were in a graveyard. Her graveyard, perhaps. Maybe when she died, she'd become one of the delicate, fluttering creatures counted by nature watchers and school children on outings.

She could fly away on the wind. Alive. Free. Real.

Brushing aside a spindly gorse, she spied a whole bush of blackberries. Fat, juicy, perfect for picking. Finally, she stopped, the bush a barrier she couldn't get past.

'About bloody time, Sal. First of all you drag us out here, then ignore us as though we're not here at all,' Audrey snapped. A cricket sprang up from the long grasses on either side of them and landed on her jeans. She ended its life with a sharp slap and a 'tsk'.

'Why'd you do that?' Sally asked, staring at the cricket's corpse on the ground.

'Do what?' Audrey asked.

Panting came from behind a bush, and Rose appeared. 'Are you two … fighting … again?' she wheezed.

The years of smoking had not been kind to her —not that she'd admit it. But the stains on her teeth, discoloration of hair and general odour overrode any protests she might have put up if Sally had bothered to point it out.

'No,' Sally said simply.

'Well, then. Now that we've stopped … for a breather, care to tell us why we're here?' Rose asked, leaning up against a thick tree trunk.

Sally knelt down to pick up the dead cricket, cupped it in her hands, then put it under a decaying log full of woodlice. 'You do know where we are?'

'Of course we do. This is the wood where dad used to come and sketch every day,' Audrey said. 'What of it?'

'He brought us here the day he died. It's been ten years since then, and we've been apart the whole time.'

Audrey crossed her arms, sighing. 'It's not like we had a choice. You were ill. We had to let the hospital take you.'

'And it obviously worked. Look at you now,' Rose added, indicating the faint silver scars that were all that was left of Sally's self-inflicted injuries.

Sally held her arm up to the beams of sunlight breaking through the treetops. The scars made her skin look like they'd been imbued with the same metallic strips in bank notes. She stretched the skin, distorting them, playing with them.

Audrey leaned over and clicked her fingers by Sally's ears. 'Hey!'

Sally jumped. 'Why didn't you ever come and see me there?' she asked softly.

Rose shrugged. 'Mum told us not to. Said it would interfere with your treatment. That, and we never quite got over you trying to set the house alight.'

'Yeah, finding out that your sister wants to murder you doesn't exactly inspire confidence,' Audrey said, brushing leaf litter off her patent boots.

Goose pimples rose on Sally's skin. The temperature had dropped. She liked the sensation of the cold reaching out to her.

'I wasn't trying to harm you, I was trying to protect you,' she told them. 'I saw a monster outside our room, so I put a candle to the rug so it couldn't cross the threshold.'

'A monster? Jeez, Sal, you're still holding on to that story? Any monsters you saw were in your head.'

'I know that, Audrey. I was a child. I was scared. Dad wasn't there to do the bogeyman dance with us, so I started seeing all kinds of things. They whispered to me in the night, taunting me.'

'God, this is crazy,' Audrey muttered, rubbing her face with her hand. 'Sal, it wasn't real. It was all psychological.'

'That doesn't mean it wasn't real for me at the time!' Sally shouted, disturbing a family of jackdaws nesting in the trees around them. They took flight, sending shadows dancing around the area. 'You asked me why I brought you here. This is one of the reasons! I needed to know if you'd talk to me again now that Mum's gone. I needed to know just how much she'd poisoned you against me.'

Rose moved from her position against the tree trunk and crossed over to Sally, taking her hands. 'Mum did anything but poison us against you. She just reinforced what we all felt. That it was better for you to be away from us. We always knew you were dad's favourite, that's why it affected you so much when he killed himself. He never gave you any clue what he was about to do. Mum tried for years to support him and make him get help, but he wouldn't. You were the only one who didn't see how he really was. To you, he was always full of life, full of energy and wanting to go off on adventures. It broke poor Mum's heart that he spared so little consideration for her when she'd done so much for him.'

Sally stepped back, knocking a few blackberries off the bush. 'You're wrong. I saw the parts of him he tried to hide all the time. But I chose to see all of him, and that included the good.' She took a breath, brushing back the long tangles of blonde hair falling in front of her face. 'He told me what he was planning. I knew when he brought us here that morning that he'd kill himself by the seven o'clock chime in the evening.'

Audrey and Rose stared at her. 'What?' Audrey asked, her voice cracking. 'Why didn't you say anything? We could have—'

'You wouldn't have stopped him. He was determined. He was happy. If I'd have told you, that would only have made him sad.'

'Oh, Sally,' Rose murmured. 'You locked the door for him, didn't you?'

Sally nodded. 'He didn't want any of us to see how he'd look after.' A butterfly drifted by her face, landing briefly on her bare arm before fluttering away again. 'The reason why his death destroyed me isn't because of what he did. It was because he didn't keep his promise. He didn't come back to get me. So I've made a decision I thought you should know about. *I'm going after him.*'

She turned, facing the bush, preparing for what was on the other side. She doubted they remembered; they'd rarely played this way. At least they'd find out now.

The Poison Spreading

'MOTHER, look at the river! All the fish are dead!'

Naida swallowed and emerged from the under-growth to see her young son standing by the river-bank, looking out at the rushing water beyond. The river, which usually gushed blue and was filled with energetic silver fish, was now a dull mud colour. The fish were lifeless, their bodies carried by nothing but the river's flow.

She had noticed the river's decline in health two days ago, when dark stains appeared within its depths, and had warned everyone not to collect water from it unless they were desperate, hoping that by now any danger to them might have passed. But it hadn't, and now their water stores were run-ning dry, even with the help of the forest's daily downpour. Something had to be done, for if there was something in the water powerful enough to kill all the fish, then how would her village stand a chance? She had to confront the Elder and force him to look beyond the needs of his sickly son, hard as that might be for him.

'Stay away from it, Ren. It's dangerous,' she said as he made to prod a stick at one of the dead fish floating by.

'But I'm thirsty, mother, and my water skin is empty.'

'Then you'll just have to wait until we find some juicy fruit, or a leaf full of dew. That will quench your thirst.'

Ren pulled a face, but Naida ignored it. Still, she understood all too well how he felt. She herself had gone without water since noon the day before in order for him and his sister to drink, and had been sustaining herself on the small collection of fleshy fruit that they had stored away.

Gathering up their empty water pots, they made their way back to the village, treading the well-known path through the undergrowth. Hearing the noise of the forest cheered Naida; the birds were calling spiritedly to one another, the primates were foraging up amongst the trees and the hum of insects filled the air, proof that not all life had been affected by the decline of the river. If there was one thing that Naida loved about the forest, it was that she was never alone there. There were always other creatures darting about, reminding her that it was home to so many.

Ren, however, had been introduced to the world outside the forest by travellers and was overcome with curiosity at the gadgets they possessed. For him, the forest that his mother loved so dearly seemed dull in comparison. Even so, he respected the life around him and helped his mother around the village, practicing their traditional ways. Soon he would start learning how to hunt with his father, though Naida could hardly believe he was old enough already. It felt like it was only a few short months since he was a babe in arms.

They reached the village an hour later, greeted by Naida's daughter, Laka. She was a few years older than Ren and not nearly so fascinated with the outside world as he was. In fact, the thought made her nervous, for she knew that there would be so many sights to see and people about that she would not be able to take it all in.

'Your water pots are empty again, Mother?' she asked, taking one from Naida and shaking it just to be sure.

'The river is still ailing. The fish are dead and the water is no longer clear. I must tell the Elder. He *has* to take note of it now.'

'The river has worsened? What will we do?' Laka asked, despair in her voice.

Naida put her hand on her daughter's shoulder. 'The Elder will know what to do, so don't alarm yourself about it,' she said, much more confidently than she felt. 'For now, help your brother gather more fruits so we may drink the juice, and ask the other children to do it for their own families. However, it would be unwise to tell them in detail just how bad the river has become until I have spoken with the Elder. There's no need to cause a panic.'

Laka nodded and went off to find her friends, trailing her brother behind her. Naida inhaled deeply. It was late afternoon; the Elder was usually seeing to his son at that time and would not take kindly to being disturbed. Perhaps she would be allowed to wait in his hut until he returned.

She made her way to the middle of the village where the Elder's hut was located. Nothing about it suggested that it belonged to him other than a small, delicate symbol carved above the entrance. It was even the same size and shape as the rest of the huts.

Naida took a breath to call inside, but before she could do so, the Elder's wife, Ayme, appeared in the doorway. 'Come in, Naida,' she smiled warmly. 'There's no need to stand outside. You know that you are always welcome here.'

Naida smiled back at her and took up her invitation. It was cool and dry, at least compared to the dense humidity outside. Ayme brought her a small cup of berry juice, and they sat drinking it in silence.

'My husband will be back shortly,' Ayme said after a while. 'These past few days have been difficult for him. Our son's condition is getting steadily worse. He fears that our only option is to take him to the outside for treatment there.'

'But how would we pay for something like that? The outside is run with money; we can't simply trade goods.'

The flap around the doorway opened and the Elder came in, looking more drawn and dishevelled that Naida had ever seen him before. 'That is something we shall discuss if the need comes to pass.' He took a swig of the juice that his wife offered him and sat down with them. 'Now Naida, what is it I can do for you? It seems we spoke only recently.'

'That was two days past, Elder. And I would not trouble you again if it wasn't so urgent,' she replied. 'Elder, my son Ren and I were down by the river to collect water not long ago. Do you remember I told you something wasn't right about it last time, and I advised everyone not to drink from it until it had cleared up? Well, this time, not only was the water discoloured, but it was murky and every fish we saw was dead.'

'So it really is too dangerous to drink, then?' Ayme said, her eyes wide. 'This is very disturbing news.'

'Now, now, let us not get ahead of ourselves. Do not forget, fish are far more sensitive creatures than we. What affects them may not affect us at all,' the Elder said, scratching his beard musingly. 'It may well be the case that some large animal has died further upstream and its remains are now polluting the water. I shall go myself and check. We should make no more assumptions until I return.'

Naida inclined her head and stood up, bowing to them both. For some reason, the Elder's words did not comfort her as much as she had been hoping. It was true that animals did sometimes die near the water and pollute it as they rotted, but she had never seen the river look like that in all her years. He had been too quick to jump to such a conclusion, and even though he said he would inspect the cause himself, she couldn't shake the feeling that he was hiding something.

She remembered that a few weeks earlier, the Elder had three outsiders visit him. He said after they'd left that they had merely been scientists, observing the natural world, but now she felt he'd been lying. But why would he? What was it that the Elder was trying to conceal from everyone?

————

After the sun had set and Laka and Ren were asleep, Naida went out into the village by herself. Her husband was out hunting and wouldn't be home for another three days, along with the rest of the hunting party. The wives of the other men in the party were all younger than Naida, and so she rarely met with them while their men were gone. Now, however, she passed them outside their huts. Despite the failing light, some still sat repairing clothes and weaving baskets, but all talked animatedly to each other.

She gave a word of greeting and they nodded in reply, but she did not feel like stopping. Instead, she planned to go to the Elder's hut again to ask if she may go with him when he was to inspect the river. When she got there, however, Ayme was alone inside, readying herself for sleep.

'Naida, I did not expect to see you again so soon,' she said, her eyes questioning.

'Forgive me, Ayme, I did not mean to disturb your rest,' Naida apologised.

The older woman shook her head. 'My dear, it is perfectly alright. You are obviously still troubled by something. Tell me, what is it?'

Naida sighed. 'I am still concerned about the river. I was hoping that the Elder would let me go with him when he inspects it so we may both see it clearly and discover the cause.'

'You suspect my husband may not be up to it?' Ayme asked, pulling her blankets around her shoulders. The night had turned cold, and her body no longer kept warmth in as it used to.

'It's not that,' Naida hesitated. 'I feel as though he is disinterested in finding the true cause. He may be right in his suspicions, and I hope that he is … but I want to be sure. I have never seen the river like that in all my life, nor have I heard anyone tell of something like this happening before.'

Ayme pursed her lips. 'I admit that I, too, feel as

though he is not as concerned as he should be. However, he has been true to his word, for already he has gone to examine it.'

'At night? But how will he see it properly? Even with a lighted torch, it will be difficult. Did you not find that strange, Ayme?' Naida said, shaking her head.

'Yes, but perhaps it is his plan to follow the riverbank a good way up and wait until the first light to see its true state,' she said, but deep lines had formed on her brow.

'How long ago did he leave?' Naida pressed.

Ayme thought for a moment. 'Just a few minutes longer than you have been here. If you are swift, then you may be able to catch up to him.'

Naida put her hand on Ayme's shoulder and thanked her, before leaving the hut as quickly as she could. She took one of the torches blazing by the storage hut and made her way down the path to the river.

She was even more cautious at night than she was in the day, as many creatures came out in the darkness, including some that could bring instant death if she were bitten or attacked. Fortunately, the torchlight made many of them scatter from her wake when she passed through, leaving her un-scathed. Ahead of her, in the distance, she could just make out the light from another torch. It must be the Elder.

She was surprised that she had caught up to

him so quickly, but then she remembered that his age had started to affect him these past few years and he was no longer the fast hunter that she had grown up watching.

He was nearing the riverbank, it was just beyond the next clump of bushes to his right, but instead of turning towards it, he carried on. Where was he going? Curious, and more than a little suspicious, she decided to follow him. She dulled her torch so that the flames flickered as low as she could get them, pursuing him further and further until she was sure he must be lost. She herself had only been this way a few times before; it was not a good place for hunting or gathering foods, so the villagers tended not to go there.

Yet the Elder's pace wasn't hesitant, but strong and confident. Ahead of him, she suddenly spied a bright light. Some of it was firelight, but the rest looked as though it was the strange unnatural lights used by people on the outside.

What were they doing here? Had they come to make a settlement, or were they just a large group of travellers like the ones who visited the village? No, she thought, they were up to something else.

As she got closer, she saw that all of the trees in the area had been cut down, and enormous pits lay there instead, great chasms so deep in the earth that looking at them was like looking into nothingness itself. Tents were scattered about them, as well as huge metal structures—machines, she remembered they were called—that stood dormant on the site. The whole area glistened with moisture, despite the fact that it had not rained for hours. Sloped as the area was, she could see the last trickles of run-off spilling downwards, in the direction of the river.

The Elder continued on, right into the heart of the light. Naida hid behind the surrounding bushes, watching as he neared a group of people sitting around a campfire. As they saw him approach, they called out behind them and another man appeared from one of the tents. His eyes darted to the Elder, and immediately his mouth broke into a wide grin, like a jaguar watching particularly easy prey before it attacked. He beckoned to a young boy by the fire, who scrambled up obediently to stand beside him.

'Ah, Elder Cirilo,' the boy said, translating the man's rushed foreign words as he energetically took the Elder's hand and shook it. 'What may we do for you on this fine evening?'

'You said that our village wouldn't be harmed,' the Elder said, sparing the man any niceties.

There was a pause as the boy explained what the Elder had said, but then the man's reply came. 'And I am true to my word, am I not? None of your villagers have been affected by our work here.' The man gestured broadly around him, the smile still spread across his face.

'But they could be,' the Elder replied. 'Our river is polluted; the water is discoloured and the fish are dead. Where are we supposed to fish, and what are we to drink from now on?'

The grinning man frowned deeply. 'I'm afraid I don't know what you're talking about. If the river is polluted, then it has nothing to do with us, I assure you,' the boy replied for him, casting a wary glance at his master.

'You lie. I know that you use strange potions to kill the plants and make the soil ready for your digging, and other such poisons in those foul things you have that cause explosions.'

The man's frown turned to a scowl and, as he instructed the boy with what to say, it was clear that the tone of his voice had dropped all its pleasantness. The boy shrank back, but his master gripped him tightly on the shoulder and forced him to address the Elder. 'I believe your son is terribly ill, is he not? Did we not promise to pay you a good sum of money to take him for treatment in the city in return for your silence?'

The Elder said nothing. Naida caught her breath, not wanting to believe what she'd just heard. Had these people really bought the Elder's silence? No, it couldn't be. Even if his son was ill, the Elder wouldn't accept money from such people ... *would* he?

'I want double,' the Elder said finally. 'Give me double what you offered and I'll leave you alone.'

'Done,' the boy said bitterly after another brief instruction, lowering his gaze so that he wouldn't have to look the Elder in the eyes. 'But there will be no exceptions after this.'

Naida couldn't stop herself. She ran out into the light, in full view of all the people sitting there. 'Elder, you can't do this! What about our village?'

'And who is this pretty one?' the boy said, though he was unwilling to use his master's lecherous tone. 'Hiding in the bushes, were we?'

'Naida, you should not be here,' the Elder said quietly. 'Please go back to the village.' He did not turn to her as he spoke, but instead chose to look blankly ahead of him.

'I will not,' Naida said firmly. 'Why are you letting these people keep you quiet with their paper money? Even if it is to save your son, how can you allow them to poison the river and risk the lives of our people?'

The Elder made no remark, as though her words had fallen on deaf ears.

'We cannot let them do this. We could all die if we let this carry on … my children could die, Elder!'

'Or you could move,' the boy said for the grinning man, whose interest in Naida had turned to disgust now that tears were wetting her cheeks. 'There are plenty of places to move your village— after all, the rainforest is rather large.'

'No,' the Elder snapped. 'Our people have lived in this village for generations. *We will not move.*' He looked up at Naida, staring at her as if seeing her for the first time. He saw the anger in her eyes and, with it, the sheer shock of his deception. He sniffed, and turned back to the grinning man. 'I have allowed you to manipulate me for too long. Why should my people have to suffer because of my selfishness? You can have your paper money back. I want you to leave, and take your machines and poisons with you!'

'Then your son will surely die,' the boy said, wincing as his master's grip on his shoulder became more intense. 'He needs treatment from the outside, treatment which a poor village such as yours can never hope to pay for.'

'We will find another way,' the Elder said. 'Come, Naida, we shall return to the village.'

He turned sharply and wordlessly, and Naida followed him back through the forest to their home. When they reached it, the Elder called for a meeting amongst the adults. Naida had not said a word on the way back, and refused to speak when the other villagers asked what was going on, disgruntled at being called on so late into the night. That was the Elder's task, his and his alone.

'My sons and daughters,' he began, addressing them all. 'I know that the hunting party has yet to return, but I feel I must speak with you most urgently.' He paused, trying to form his words. 'I have been lying to you all.'

The people whispered in shock and Ayme fell weakly against the walls of the hut. Naida went to

Ayme's side and let the older woman lean on her shoulder.

'Several weeks ago, some outsiders came to speak with me. I told you that they were people known as scientists that study the natural world. They were not. These people want to destroy part of the forest so that they can dig for minerals beneath the earth, to sell for their precious paper money. They told me that if I remained silent about their plans, then they would pay for my son to be treated by the healers on the outside. I am ashamed to admit that I accepted and, even today, when I found that their methods were polluting the river, I went to them not to ask them to leave, but to ask for more money for my son in return for my continued silence. They accepted and, if it hadn't been for Naida, I would have left satisfied and risked all of your lives by doing so.'

The villagers were too stunned at his words to speak, staring at him in silence. When finally they registered what he had said, a great uproar broke out. The crowd shouted and jostled against each other in a wave of fury and betrayal. The Elder endured their insults, and so foul were they that Naida was astounded he did not protest even once.

Then a young woman sprinted into the crowd from the hut where the Elder's son was housed, heading straight for Naida and Ayme. She whispered something to Ayme, and though Naida couldn't hear it over the roar of the crowd, Ayme's reaction gave the message away immediately.

She let out a cry of despair that silenced everyone, and as they turned to her, they knew just as Naida did that the only cause could be that her son was dead. It rang through the night, lasting only seconds, but to everyone present, feeling like an eternity.

With his face turning ashen, the Elder dropped to his knees. 'It is over then,' he said, his voice quiet at first, but becoming louder with each word. 'These people who wish to poison our river and dig up the land now have no power over me. They cannot play to my weakness anymore. I will bury our son and grieve for him, but then I will fight. *We* will fight. I and a few others will journey to the outside and seek assistance from those who are knowledgeable on such matters. I will not lay down and let these people threaten our way of life anymore.'

He took a breath and went to Ayme's side, his body trembling along with hers. 'But now, on this night, I will say no more. Forgive me, but I must say goodbye to my son.' They parted from the crowd and disappeared into the hut where their son's body lay, and for the rest of that night the only sound that was to be heard in the village was Ayme's sobs.

Naida felt a sadness that was deeper than any she had experienced before. Though she did not want to admit it, she understood why the Elder had gambled their lives for that of his son's. If it had been one of her own children, then she knew she would have been swayed just as easily. It was this, more than anything, that caused the guilt she now felt eating away at her. But nothing could be done now. Death had dealt its cold hand and freed the Elder from his turmoil, forcing him to move forwards.

She walked slowly back to her own hut, slipping through the doorway to see her son and daughter deep asleep, wrapped up under their blankets. She knelt down and put a hand on each of their heads, humming softly.

Chasing the outsiders from the forest and purifying the river would be no easy task, but if the villagers stood strong, they would do it. She was sure of it.

Numbered Pages

IVAN STEPPED out of the taxi, handing some notes to the driver after fumbling in his wallet, and looked up at the tall, towered building that was Waverick Institute for Boys.

It was a miniature castle to his eyes, with all the original stonework on show and surrounded by fields and pastures, far removed from the schools he'd taught at in London.

Gathering up his suitcases with a small gulp, he made his way over to the intricate metal gates, seeing an intercom on the side of the wall next to them and pressing it. It hissed, as though it had been a long time since its last use, then a low yet distinctly feminine voice came through it.

'May I help you?' the speaker asked.

Ivan cleared his throat. 'Yes, my name is Ivan Cornersberg, the new English teacher,' he replied, feeling a quiver fill his throat that was beyond his control.

'Ah, yes, I was told that you would be arriving today. Please stand back while I open the gates.'

Ivan did so, not a moment before the large gates jolted apart, squeaking on their hinges. Once the gap was wide enough for him to walk through, he picked up his suitcases once again and made his way down the long, serpentine pathway, edged almost to perfection with yellow stone slabs which separated it from the large area of lawn either side.

He reached the door of the main entrance, just as impressive as the gates had been, and used the cast iron knocker to knock three times. He heard the knock echo through the hall beyond and, after half a minute, the door opened, revealing a butler dressed in a black tailcoat and trousers, with a pocket watch chain hanging across one side of his waistcoat.

'Good morning, sir,' the butler said pleasantly, standing aside to let Ivan in. 'My name is Francis and the headmaster has bid me to welcome you to Waverick Institute for Boys. He informed me that I am to be of every possible service to you as long as you are employed here.'

'Thank you,' Ivan said, marvelling at the butler's fine suit. Compared to that, he felt rather shabby, dressed in his tweed jacket and plain trousers. He'd never heard of a butler working in a school before, but then he *was* in the country. Perhaps that was the norm out here. 'Where might I find the headmaster? I have an appointment with him this afternoon.'

'I'm afraid he is teaching at the moment, sir, but I shall take you to his office where you may wait until the bell rings for luncheon.'

The butler picked up Ivan's suitcases, his face twitching at the weight. He led Ivan down a straight long hall, carpeted in a rich red that made the English teacher feel as though he was sinking with every step he took. The butler turned sharply to the right just before they reached the end, down a smaller hall Ivan wouldn't have noticed by himself.

The headmaster's office was located there, a single door standing out proudly against the stonework of the walls. The butler took out a small brass key and put it to the lock, hearing it click before withdrawing it. He opened the door and led Ivan inside, placing his suitcases next to a tall bookshelf filled with tomes on all sorts of topics.

Ivan scanned some of their titles. *An Astronomer's Guide to the Northern Sky, From Broth to Brunch: Notes by Acclaimed Chefs on Popular Dishes, Military Tactics of the Past One Hundred Years, Criminology for Writers: Behind a Killer's Eyes.* A shiver went down Ivan's spine at the last one, though it might have been caused by the watchful gaze of the butler, who took the moment to cough.

'Please wait in here until the headmaster arrives. I'm afraid I must lock you in, however, for some of the boys have taken to sneaking in here lately and upsetting the headmaster's desk,' he said, his tone polite yet with a definite edge to it. 'By your leave, sir, I shall depart.'

Ivan nodded. 'Yes, thank you, I'll be fine,' he said, sitting down in a velvet covered armchair. The butler bowed low and left the room, locking it as promised. Ivan looked around, taking in the headmaster's leather chair, and the desk in front of it, which was carved out of one solid piece of mahogany. There was a small box upon it, made of cherry wood and inlaid with what looked like ivory.

Ivan hoped it wasn't; with all the news of elephants nearing extinction due to poachers shooting them for their tusks, he felt it would be in rather poor taste. He was tempted to examine it to put his mind at rest if nothing else, but as he got up, he heard a key placed into the lock and swiftly sat down again.

The door swung open and a short man with his face hidden from view by a large pile of books shuffled his way inside. One of the books toppled off, and Ivan leapt up to before it hit the floor.

'Ah, thank you,' the man said, not looking at him and putting the pile of books on the desk. 'I was hoping I could manage, but …'

He turned around and his ruddy face broke into a smile. 'Ah, Ivan! I wasn't sure if you would be here yet. I've just been teaching one of the classes that you'll be taking over. Lively one, that,' he said, sitting down in his chair.

'Didn't the butler tell you I'd arrived?' Ivan asked.

'Butler?' the headmaster said. 'Oh, you mean Francis? He's not really a butler, you know, he's actually our caretaker. Bit of an odd one, dressing up like that and speaking in such a formal manner, but he's good at his job and, surprisingly, the boys take no notice of him. So we just leave him to it now.'

'Oh, I see,' said Ivan, sitting back in the armchair. He studied the headmaster. Though he hadn't seen his brother-in-law properly since the incident, Ivan thought he looked more overworked than usual. His face, though still broad, was thinner than it had been and his hairline had greatly receded.

Still, Ivan knew that he'd changed as well. No one could go through what he had over the past year and stay the same.

'Now, down to business,' the headmaster said, resting his hands on the desk in front of him and crossing his fingers. 'I know you've had a lot of trouble finding work recently, and I'm sure … given the circumstances, it's been hard living alone.

'As I told you over the phone, Mr Summers, our previous English teacher, became ill just before the start of term and had to leave. Now, I've been teaching his class for the past few weeks since then, but with my own work to see to, it's proving somewhat difficult. I know you agreed to take the position when I called you, but I wanted to show you Waverick before you made your final decision. As you have no doubt already seen, this is no London school. Here we take the needs of every student very seriously and so our classes are small, with ten students being the maximum in each class. How do you feel about this?'

'Well, I'm sure it'll take me a while to get used to it, but this may be the very thing I need,' Ivan replied.

'Glad to hear it,' the headmaster said, smiling. 'As we are a boarding school, I should tell you that only one or two of our students go home for the holidays, as most of their parents work overseas. I will warn you now that they can be a handful, though if you start with the right approach, they can be just as eager to learn as any. Are you still happy to take on the position after hearing this?'

Ivan nodded. 'Of course I am. If I'm honest, Thomas, then just being out of London and being allowed to teach again is a weight off my shoulders.' He sat for a moment, thinking. 'I must ask you, though, do the students and other staff know about what happened?'

A small crease appeared on the headmaster's brow. 'Yes, they do, but I have told them all that I have the utmost confidence in you and had I any doubt of your innocence, then I would have been the first one to turn away from you.'

Ivan breathed a long sigh of relief. 'Well, at least I don't have to hide anything.'

'Of course, that would be an intimidating situation for anyone to have to walk into,' the headmaster said. He opened a drawer in his desk and took out a sheet of paper, headed at the top with a crest depicting an eagle with a rabbit in its talons, Waverick Institute's crest. He pushed it in front of Ivan and handed him a pen. 'Here is your official contract. If you have any questions, please feel free to ask.'

Ivan scanned the document quickly. It looked like a standard teacher's contract, like any other he had signed. He took up the pen and scribbled his signature and the date at the bottom, before passing it back to the headmaster.

'Excellent,' the headmaster said, taking it and putting it back in his drawer. 'I'll just give Francis a ring so he can show you up to your room. Oh, I will ask you not to call me Thomas in front of the students, though. You must address me as Headmaster. They tend to get cocky if they know your first name,' he added, before picking up the receiver to an old-fashioned rotary phone on a shelf behind him. Ivan smiled. He hadn't seen one of those since his visits to his grandmother's as a child.

As the headmaster turned away, Ivan took a moment to check his own phone, an old Nokia that had served him faithfully these past ten years. The signal bar at the top was empty. He ought to have known as much; he hadn't seen any signal towers at all on his ride down here. He sighed, knowing that it was just one of the things he would have to get used to, but knew there were benefits to it, too. After all, with no signal, he couldn't receive any hate messages left by people he didn't know that had somehow gotten hold of his number.

'Francis will be with us in a moment,' the headmaster said, putting down the receiver and turning back to him. 'Want a drink while you wait?' he asked, opening a cabinet to his side that was stocked full of brandy.

Ivan laughed. 'I think it's a little early in the day for me,' he said, watching the headmaster pour himself a glass.

'Suit yourself. You might think differently after you've given your first class.'

A moment later, there was a knock on the door and, at the headmaster's command, Francis, the butler—or caretaker, whatever he was—came into the room and bowed to them both.

'You summoned me, Headmaster?' he asked.

'Yes, I did,' the headmaster said, eyeing Francis' attire and shaking his head. 'Would you please show Ivan up to his room?'

'If that is your wish, Headmaster,' Francis replied and, picking up Ivan's suitcases once more, strode out of the room.

Ivan jumped up to follow him before he headed out of sight.

'I'll see you at dinner tonight, Ivan,' the head-master called to him with a wave.

The next morning, throwing his clothes on haphazardly after realising that he'd set his alarm half an hour later than he was supposed to, Ivan rushed out of his room and down the staircase taking him to the entrance hall. He looked across at the four corridors leading away from it, trying to remember which one led to the dining hall. Taking a guess, he chose the one leading left and followed it.

Seeing the sturdy wooden door at the end, he sighed with relief. He went in, wearing what he hoped was a friendly, yet authoritative expression as the crowd of students looked up at him from their breakfast plates. He had seen them briefly at dinner the previous night, but had retired early due to a sudden headache.

The other teachers, whom the headmaster had told him usually arrived at dinner half an hour later than himself and the students, due to the marking they always did after class, had not met him yet and so also watched him with curiosity as he made his way up to their table. He sat in the empty seat next to the headmaster and his secretary, the middle-aged woman who had answered the intercom when he had first arrived.

'Sorry I'm late,' he apologised to them all as he shuffled into his chair.

'Not to worry,' a man sitting opposite him said, with a finely trimmed beard and glasses. 'I remember my first day here. I was so unprepared that I walked into a geography class and tried to teach them maths. It was only until I was halfway through my explanation of Pythagoras's theorem that I realised Miss James here was waiting patiently for me to stop talking so that she could teach her class.' He nodded to the young woman next to Ivan and smiled at her.

'I remember that,' she said, also smiling. 'But I believe the best award goes to Mr Heathers, at the end there. He teaches biology, and muddled up his explanation of reproduction so badly that the boys kept getting meiosis confused with mitosis and it took him the rest of the term to get them to relearn it correctly. Of course, that's partly because his eyesight is so bad that he didn't realise their mistake for a good few weeks.'

'What's this?' Mr Heathers said from the end of the table. Ivan saw that he was an elderly man in his seventies, well past the age of any of the teachers he'd worked with in the city. 'What's all this talk of my toes?'

Miss James rolled her eyes. 'He's also quite deaf,' she said to Ivan despairingly.

They finished breakfast and the headmaster led Ivan to the English classroom. To his surprise, the students were already there, despite it being at least two minutes until the bell. He recognised a number of them from the breakfast hall.

'Class, I am pleased to introduce you to your

new English teacher, Mr Cornersberg. I assure you that he is much more knowledgeable than I am on this subject, as I'm sure you were all hoping.'

A boy at the back, with his tie done up roughly, sniggered. 'We don't mind, Headmaster,' he called out. 'At least with you, we got away with messing up our usage of there, their, and they're.'

The headmaster looked at Ivan with a pained expression. 'Spelling and grammar have always been a weakness of mine,' he admitted. 'Now then, I suppose I should leave you to it?'

'Thank you, Headmaster,' Ivan said, giving him a nod as he left the room. He turned to his class, anxiety biting his insides—a sensation he hadn't felt since his training days. As he'd been advised by his therapist, it was quite normal to feel that way after months of avoiding all human contact. He just had to breathe and focus on his lesson plan.

'As the headmaster informed you, my name is Mr Cornersberg. I'll write that on the board for you so that you can write it correctly in your books.'

He turned to the blackboard and chalked his name on it, unused to the feel now that most schools preferred white boards and projector screens. Somehow, it felt nice to be using such basic equipment again, without all the fuss of technology.

'Now,' he said, rubbing the chalk from his fingers onto his black trousers without thinking. A few of the class smirked at the white prints he left. 'The headmaster has given me some notes left by your teacher from last year, Mr Summers, I believe. According to them, you have already done one piece of coursework analysing *Far From The Madding Crowd* by Thomas Hardy, yet he feels that most of your pieces were not strong enough to include in your GCSE portfolios. Not to worry, though, as we'll be working on a different piece of work that you might engage with slightly more. Tell me, has anyone heard of *To Kill a Mocking Bird* by Harper Lee?'

The class progressed smoothly and, as Ivan had suspected, the boys latched onto the themes much easier than with the previous book they'd studied. He'd brought enough copies of it for them to have one each and by the end of the class, they had covered the whole of the first chapter and had time to analyse it, too.

As the bell rang for the switch to second period, the class left and Ivan collected the copies of the book and stacked them on his desk, preparing another set for the year above them, this time Shakespeare's *Othello*. He put a copy on each desk before returning to his own and counting the copies of *To Kill a Mockingbird*, making sure they were all there.

As he picked up the top copy, a note slid out from under the cover, accompanied by a newspaper clipping.

Without having to look, Ivan knew what the clipping said. 'Body of pregnant wife found cradled in husband's arms.' There was a photo of their wedding day, then one of just his Julia.

Tentatively, he unfolded the note. The word 'Murderer' was spelt out on it using the foil covering of a paracetamol pill strip.

Seeing it brought him to his knees. How had they known? That detail had never been released to the public. No one but the police and the pathologist who had done the post-mortem knew. They hadn't even told Thomas.

What if whoever sent it suspected what the paracetamol had really been? But that was impossible, not a single person could sniff *that* out.

Reassured, Ivan scrunched up the clipping and note. He'd burn it in the fireplace in his room later. For now, he had a class to teach.

Retracing the Mind

MY FATHER USED to make flutes by hand.

Every day, I would watch him choose the material; some days it would be wood, others clay or bamboo.

He spent hours carving and shaping just a single one, never happy unless it was perfectly in tune, with a voice that would ring out through his studio and into the streets beyond. Often, he would find imperfections in his work and cast them out into a great skip he had solely for that purpose, before starting on a new flute with even more enthusiasm, striving to make it perfect.

As he worked, he used to tell me that music could soothe the soul and heal the mind from any illness or depression, allowing both the musician and audience to free themselves of the worries of modern living. He said it was for this reason that only the most exceptional flutes he made would pass his approval—for how could one make fine music without a fine instrument?

When he wasn't looking, I would take one of the discarded flutes, walk down to the woods, and play it for hours until suppertime. I could never play as well as he could, but these flutes he simply threw away because they weren't up to his standard sounded beautiful anyway. Whether or not they soothed my soul, I don't know, but they did calm me after a difficult day at school.

As the years went by, father threw out more and more flutes, never happy with what he was working on. At first, I thought he was striving too much for perfection, but the day after my youngest daughter was born, he was diagnosed with early onset dementia.

The condition progressed rapidly, and he was taken into care barely a year after his diagnosis. It was a hard decision, but my mother could no longer look after him, and with my growing family and work at the museum of Natural History, I couldn't either.

Visiting him was difficult. The man I knew was no longer there. He could barely remember his name, let alone his love for music, and I would often leave close to tears.

Years later, after the museum had received a large shipment of artefacts, I discovered an unusual find. It was fashioned like some of the clay ocarinas father used to make, but it had two sound holes, meaning there were two chambers inside that made it possible to play two notes at once. The description that came with it was that it had been made by the Incas in Pre-Columbian Peru, and was thought to have been used to achieve a higher spiritual awareness.

As I held it, I found a strong urge to show it to him. Usually, the artefacts we received were only allowed outside the museum for transportation to other museums, but my boss knew about my father's condition and let me take it to him, strictly as a one-off between the two of us. And, under no circumstances, was I to tell anyone about it.

When I arrived at the care home later that evening, I found father arguing with one of the assistants, adamant that they were poisoning his food. I broke in quickly, apologising for his behaviour, and took him into his private room.

Deciding that he had calmed down enough, I took out the ancient flute from my bag and carefully unwrapped it. Up to that point, he had been staring at the wall, but as I put the flute to my lips and blew into it, hazarding a guess at where to place my fingers, he turned to look at me. I continued to play, lifting my fingers to change the clear, strong notes coming out of it and, gently, I saw a spark come back into his eyes.

'Where did you get that?' he asked.

I almost dropped the flute on the floor. It was

the first coherent sentence he had spoken in years, and I knew at once that he was lucid. I told him what little I knew about it, and he took it off me and examined the instrument, muttering a run-down of it as he did so.

Then he put it to his lips and played it himself. At that moment, I finally understood what he'd been telling me, for the sound coming out of it made every anxiety currently ruling my body disappear. My mind was quietened and I was more alive than I had been since childhood. I knew he felt it too, and for hours afterwards we sat and talked like we used to before he was ill.

As the evening drew on, we drifted into slumber. When I awoke the next morning, still propped in the armchair by his bed, my eyes caught sight of his still face, a smile carrying the same accomplishment as those he'd had after crafting his finest instruments.

In his hand, the ancient flute still lay, innocuous, and I knew then he'd died the man I remembered, not the shadow the years had made him.

I returned the flute to the museum after I'd informed everyone of his passing. My boss took it back without question, displaying it prominently for all the world to see. As I caught my reflection in the glass of the display, the last tune my father had played echoed in my head, and on the flute's shiny surface, his face appeared.

It winked once, and was gone.

The Face

THERE IS a face in the tree, under the bark, swelling into a bulbous mask. Not frozen in place, but with the ability to ripple up the branches and into the leaves, pushing forth to stop in the soft white flowers. There it waits, until an unsuspecting bee or wasp lands on the delicate petals searching for pollen. Then: gulp!

The insect is swallowed whole by the face, with not even a furred black leg or crystal-like wing left as proof that it was ever there.

Once full, the face retreats down to the roots of the tree and hides, safe among the moss and soft soil where the smell of petrichor can overpower its own scent. Away from the keen senses of the woodland huntresses, with their sharp, hooked nails and unrivalled speed at climbing trees. Dryads, the protectors of the wood.

They have been chasing the face for more years than it can remember, ever since it crept away from them one night when it was little more than a babe.

You see, the face was once a male dryad, and it is well known amongst all dryad kind, from those in the great wilds to those in small country woods, that a male babe is an omen that the wood will soon die.

Fearing that her sisters would turn on the babe, its mother placed it by the road where humans often passed by, in the hopes that it would be found and cared for by them (for so similar to human young are dryad offspring at birth, that it is easy to mistake one for the other, and a year of feeding a dryad babe on human food would cause the simi-larity to become permanent).

But seeking its mother's breast as all infants do, the babe crawled back to the dryads' dwellings in search of her. There, it was discovered by the dryad queen who, repulsed by all it represented, sought to gauge it to death with her savage nails.

Yet the Earth did not wish the babe to die. Swallowing it up into a nest the dryad queen could not penetrate, the Earth granted it the power to be-come one with the woods, with only its face ever visible.

Once its metamorphosis was complete, the Earth released it. The babe used its new form to elude the queen, and rippled across the ground and out of sight. Angered and fearful of what it might do, the queen ordered her sisters to seek it out and kill it on sight.

Soon after, the trees of the dryads' dwellings began to fade. They could not see it was their own neglect doing so, and nothing to do with the babe. For the babe was now a face, and no longer a dryad at all. While the trees of the dryads died, the trees the face inhabited thrived, growing tall and strong for another year.

Even now, the dryads are blind to their neglect. Yet so many of their birth-trees have died that their numbers have dwindled, and it will not be long before the face is free of their hunt and can live its life fully as the woods' true protector.

The Lowlands

MOTHER'S SCENT was still fresh in the den when I awoke. Light was creeping in through the gaps in the leaves that sheltered us. I blinked. It was strange; day had come, yet Mother had gone out and left me alone. She had never done that before, not even at night when she went out foraging. I was *always* with her.

I stood up and stretched my front legs, shifting my weight to my hind, and then shook myself. She couldn't have been gone very long, else her scent wouldn't be that strong. Should I go out and look for her? I wanted to, but then I remembered what she'd said about going out during the day. Not all the creatures of the forest were friendly. There were predators whose fangs and claws would rip through my hide with ease.

I asked why they would want to do such a thing,

but she hadn't answered. All she'd said was they didn't eat plants like we did. Even Sister, who was old enough to shelter on her own, wouldn't say any more.

Thinking for a moment, I scratched my front leg with my back foot. Maybe Sister knew where Mother had gone. Her den was only a short way from ours. Even if there were predators about, it was near enough for me to reach quickly and I was a fast runner.

I walked towards the entrance of our den, a thickly leafed bush that was flexible enough to squeeze through, but springy enough to bounce back into shape to shield us from outsiders. I poked my snout through the leaves and sniffed. There were no strange scents lingering in the air, so I pushed my head through a bit more and looked around. Nothing was there. It was safe.

Exiting the den, I surveyed the area again, but there was still no movement anywhere. Even so, I ran over to Sister's den, making a short call to let her know I was there. There was no reply. I went in, squeezing through the bushes. Sister was gone, too. Had she gone with Mother, or for some reason of her own?

I pawed the ground. What should I do? I was all alone, and there was no sign of where Mother or Sister had gone. I trembled, wondering if I'd ever feel Mother's warm body huddled against me again. *Why had she left?*

A strange scent entered my nostrils, making my snout itch. With it came a strange grey cloud that irritated my eyes and scratched my throat, making me cough. I had never smelt anything that gave me *that* reaction. I didn't like it.

The smell grew stronger and the strange cloud became thicker. It was so dense that I couldn't breathe. In a moment of panic, I ran out of Sister's den into the open, but even there, there was no escape.

I ran and ran, heart hammering and lungs burning, as the thick grey cloud continued to surround me. I couldn't see clearly or smell anything other than that awful scent.

The trees and bushes were being attacked by a strange orange and yellow creature, with many long tongues that turned the leaves black and withered. The creature was hot and it crackled angrily. I backed away from it, but it was attacking the trees behind me, too. There was no way I could get away.

In desperation, I cried out for Mother, a long wailing cry that could just be heard above the creature's loud crackling. I listened out for her reply, but it didn't come. I tried again, louder this time. The yellow creature was getting closer, in a few minutes it would get me.

Then, quiet at first, but growing stronger, I heard Mother's answering call. I called again, repeating myself so she could find me through the grey cloud.

Just as the yellow creature closed in, she broke through and led me away. We didn't stop until we found a place where the cloud hadn't spread, but even then my eyes hadn't cleared properly.

Exhausted, my legs gave way and I dropped to the ground; excitement and fear making me quiver so much that I could feel my very hide shaking. Mother nuzzled me, rubbing her snout all over, making sure I wasn't hurt.

―――

We wandered for days, trying to find our way back to the den. The grey cloud had completely cleared now, but the acrid scent, though faint, still remained. None of the trees had survived, and in their place stood only blackened branches and grey powder. Even the pond where we foraged was full of it, making it impossible to eat. I was very weak, and Mother suffered too. She hadn't eaten in so long that her milk had run dry and she couldn't feed me.

As for Sister, we found no sign of her, nor anyone else. I began to think we were the only ones left, but Mother told me not to fret. Our kind always found each other.

The sound of a twig snapping echoed around us. We froze. A tall creature standing on two legs was watching us. Its face was hidden by a black cover, but its eyes showed through. The skin around them was pale, almost the colour of wood underneath the bark. It held a long, odd shaped branch at us, and when the creature moved, the branch spat something hard at Mother's shoulder with an angry snap that made my ears ring. She screamed out in pain and ran. I followed, barely managing to keep up.

We passed the dead, dry ground to a place where the trees were still green and the air fresh. Eventually, Mother's pace slowed down to a jog, then a walk.

She moved slower and slower, until finally it was too much for her and she fell down on her side. Her breath was shallow and fast, her eyes barely open. I cried again, trying to get her to stand up. Again and again I urged her, but she just couldn't do it.

A rustling behind me made me turn, thinking that the creature was back. It was—or at least it looked like it. This one was slightly smaller and more of its skin was showing, though it was the colour of fallen leaves. It carried no branch, but I shied away from it all the same.

'Bob. Bob!' came the strange sound from its lips.

More rustling came from behind it and another one appeared, bigger, but still with empty hands. 'My gosh, it's a baby tapir. And behind it, look!' it said.

'I think it's the mother,' the first one said, creeping forward. 'It looks injured.'

I whimpered, but it only made the creature come closer.

'I think I'll get the crate. There's a vet back at the village. Maybe we can help it,' the larger one said, before disappearing into the bushes.

The first one continued watching us until the larger one came back, carrying a small den made out of unusual twigs. It put it on the floor in front of me, and I could see that there was some kind of food inside. My hunger was so strong that I took a step forwards.

Before I knew it, the small creature was behind me, chasing me into the den. I discovered the twigs it was made of were cold and hard and didn't smell like trees at all.

The creature picked up the den and carried me off. Mother was still lying on the ground, not moving. I could just make out her belly rising and falling with her breath. I cried as I was taken out of sight of her. The creature carrying me made a soft cooing noise. Was it trying to calm me?

It put me down on a wide, flat piece of stone, which was balanced on strange, round black things. I was left there by myself for a while, shivering against the cold twigs of the den. Then both the creatures appeared, holding Mother between them. They put her next to me on something soft, and the smaller creature sat with her, rubbing its hand along her belly.

The other moved to the front of the stone out of my sight. There was a deep growl, and suddenly we were moving through the forest at a pace faster than I could ever dream of running. I lost my balance several times, and each time the creature sitting by Mother put her hand through the cold twigs of the den and held me steady, making that strange cooing noise.

It didn't seem like it wanted to hurt me, and Mother had always said a dangerous creature would attack at the first chance it got. These creatures had had plenty of chances to attack me, but they hadn't.

But what were they, and why did they want mother and me?

———

I woke up to find that I was no longer on the moving, growling stone. Instead, I was in an open area full of plants, with a pool I could swim in and drink from. There was something unusual about it, though. The plants weren't the ones that we would usually eat, and there were no algae in the pool. I looked closer at where I was, and noticed that it wasn't as open as I thought. A wall of tall twigs grew around the area, with gaps large enough to see through but too small to fit through. I was trapped again.

Mother was nowhere to be found either, nor the strange creatures that had brought us here. I was about to cry out for her, but someone called to me instead. I turned around. Sister!

She was there with me inside the wall of twigs. I ran to her and she nuzzled me. I returned it, but then I saw the strange tall creature who had sat with Mother, looking at us over the wall.

'Bob, I think these two know each other. Look at their behaviour,' it said, as the other one came to stand with it.

'The vet did say that the bigger one there was still a youngster. Perhaps they're from the same mother,' that one said.

'How is she?' the first one asked.

'She seems okay, the bullet only grazed her. She collapsed from hunger, not the wound, so the vet has her on a drip for now. He said she'll be back on the mend in a few days and we'll be able to release them,' the second said.

'But they can't go back to where they were! They burnt the whole area for the new plantation. We just about managed to stop them from burning another hundred acres,' the first exclaimed.

'We'll have to release them further down from where they were. They might not like it, but it's better than being shot by the plantation guards.'

———

Three days passed while Sister and I waited, being looked at by the strange creatures. At first, I was concerned, but I grew to ignore them unless they brought food.

On the evening of the third day, to our joy, Mother was put inside the wall with us. She was still weak, but she could now stand and give me milk again.

After another week went by, we were put on the strange growling stone again, each of us in our own small den. It moved quickly as before, but it did not take us back to our home. The area where the creatures finally let us go was similar enough, but the trees were in different places and the pools we foraged in were larger than the ones we were used to.

There were others of our kind there, some as young as me. I ran with them, playing as our mothers and sisters ate.

It wasn't our home, but maybe it *could* be.

Mirror Water

I GAZE through the frozen aquamarine wall that
has been my constant companion for so many centuries. It reflects my dishevelled form, but I can also
see through it to the tree-covered mountains beyond. Not for the first time, I wonder how it is that
no one knows the ice, and myself, are here.

Travellers and merchants regularly drive past in
their wagons, but they never even spare it a glance.
Of course, any horses and livestock they have with
them all give the ice as wide a berth as their masters
will allow, but the humans pay them no heed.

Sometimes I think I understand, for though my
original and current form is human, I have lived the
lives of many species in between. It was only as my
first human life closed to an end and my form quite
unexpectedly changed into a beast—an arctic fox, I
believe—did I see this icy wall for what it truly is. A

single layer of hardened Mirror Water, barely an inch thick, yet as resistant to force as eight feet of ice.

The curious thing: Mirror Water is never of natural origin. It is always drawn up by those who seek it, and those who seek it have not once revealed themselves. In any case, *who* raised it isn't important. *Why* it was raised—now, that's the real question.

But no matter how long I ponder it, I can't come up with an answer. The Mirror Water encloses nothing but a few rocks, petrified trees and a large, vacant cave (which, I confess, I have lived in for several centuries; I know, I know, there aren't any predators here and the temperature is constant, but the cave has a rather 'homey' feel).

And now, intruding on my quiet day, the ground beyond the wall crunches as someone hurries over the ice-covered flora. Probably another merchant or a persistent hungry predator scouting for any scraps it can find.

Alas, my interest is piqued, and I trundle closer to see what it is. It's midwinter out there, and though I can't tell exactly how cold it is, for nothing, not even a breeze permeates the Mirror Water; it's clear that the conditions outside are in no way welcoming for anything.

Barefoot and dressed in rags, a young boy scurries towards me. I have to wonder how the sorry creature survived the distance between here and the village. Curiously, he isn't shivering. In fact, he seems to be ignoring the weather completely.

He's approaching fast and I wait for him to crash into the Mirror Water, but he doesn't. Instead, he stops, raises his head as though to examine the sheer scale of it, and smiles. What's with this kid? After all this time, is he someone can actually *see* it?

He places his hand flat on the wall. It hisses, and a boy-sized hole appears in it. He steps through; I stare at him.

He stares back, taking in every detail of my slim, naked body (when you live alone for as long as I have, the modesty of normal humans seems foolish). He laughs, and gasping for breath, says, 'You're really here! I was afraid you might have perished long ago, before I had a chance to retrieve you!' His jubilation is so great that he starts dancing around in a circle.

'Forgive my interruption,' I say, irritated by his loudness in my normally peaceful enclosure, 'but may I ask just one thing? Who the hell *are* you?'

The laughter dies on his lips. 'You don't know? I thought they explained everything when they brought you here.'

'Brought me here? I remember being hit on the head, bound and gagged, and then waking up with the Mirror Water fully formed and cutting me off from everything I knew. It was a long time ago, but my memory hasn't failed,' I reply bitterly.

'Oh. That wasn't how I'd planned it at all,' he

says, pulling his tufted hair. 'Perhaps I should start from the beginning. I am your master, Phin, and I had you brought here for protection. The Mirror Water was for your benefit, I never meant for it to banish you from the world—at least not for this long.'

'Yes, eight hundred years *is* rather a long time,' I say sourly. 'And what do you mean, you're my "master"? I'm no servant, kid.'

'Guardian, then. And I'm no child. I'm what's known as a Rememberer. So are you.' He notices me shiver and turns back to the hole he made in the wall. He runs his hand down it and it seals shut again like a zipper.

I goggle at him. 'A Rememberer? You do realise that I have no idea what that means? And if you are my … guardian, then I think you rather failed at your task.'

My comment makes him look guilty. Serves him right, the little wretch.

'Well, firstly, a Rememberer is a being who lives through the ages, taking many different forms and keeping watch over the world to try and prevent mistakes being repeated. There aren't many of us. Including myself and my own master, you're the only other. You were young back then and living so close to the war zone that I had to keep you safe. It was only supposed to be for a few weeks, while we helped negotiate a treaty between the nations. But I was captured instead, a slave until the final descendant of my imprisoner died.

'My master tried to free me many times, but he was beaten and hunted no matter what form he took. He's waiting at the village now, hoping to meet you.'

I try not to snort. The abruptness of this whole situation is making me giddy to the point of hysteria. I have to sit down. How can he possibly think that I can take this all in, after so many years of silence?

'So you say I'm like you. A … Rememberer. What possible use can I be? I've been trapped in here, unable to see the world.'

'Are you joking? You must have been staring through this wall every day for centuries. You can see the mountains, the town, travellers coming and going, diseases that ravage the flora and fauna—the knowledge you've built up is surely substantial. Far more than I have gained in that period. So, will you come with me out into the world? We do need you.'

He holds his hand out to me. After all these years, I can finally *leave* this place? I look around, and then back at him. 'Under one condition,' I say. 'Never try to "protect" me again.'

He gulps at the severity of my tone as I loom over him. My body may be thin and weak at present, but at least I'm taller than he is.

'Understood,' he mumbles.

Dear reader,

We hope you enjoyed reading *When The Bard Came Visiting*. Please take a moment to leave a review, even if it's a short one. Your opinion is important to us.

Discover more books by Kathryn Rossati at

https://www.nextchapter.pub/authors/kathryn-wells-fantasy-author

Want to know when one of our books is free or discounted? Join the newsletter at

http://eepurl.com/bqqB3H

Best regards,

Kathryn Rossati and the Next Chapter Team

You might also like:
Broken Soul by Joshua Buller

To read the first chapter for free, please head to:
https://www.nextchapter.pub/books/broken-soul

About the Author

Kathryn Rossati is a writer of fantasy, children's fiction, short stories and poetry.

Her interest in writing developed at a young age when she sought to archive all the adventures that magically formed in her head, a result of being on the autistic spectrum and having an image-heavy thought process.

She currently runs a blog where she posts poetry, short stories, book reviews and writing advice. Some of her earlier works were published under the pen name Kathryn Wells.

Her favourite authors are Diana Wynne Jones, Suzanne Collins, Jonathan Stroud, Neil Gaiman, Garth Nix, J. K. Rowling, and David Eddings, to name but a few.

For more information and a complete list of her published works, please visit her website:

http://www.kathrynrossati.co.uk

When The Bard Came Visiting
ISBN: 978-4-86747-808-0
Large Print

Published by
Next Chapter
1-60-20 Minami-Otsuka
170-0005 Toshima-Ku, Tokyo
+818035793528

26th May 2021

Lightning Source UK Ltd.
Milton Keynes UK
UKHW040817150621
385545UK00004B/449